XV: (FIFTEEN)

WAR OF ROSES BOOK 1

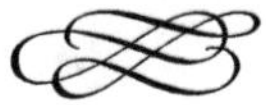

LANA SKY

XV: (Fifteen)

XV: (Fifteen) By Lana Sky

Copyright © 2019 by Lana Sky
All rights reserved.

ACKNOWLEDGMENTS

Mickey, thank you so very much for taking the time to help me perfect this draft. As always, your feedback and expertise have been invaluable. Thank you, Charity for applying the final touches on this draft.

Thanks so much to everyone who supported this draft along the way, including the many beta readers who provided encouragement along the way! Please keep in mind that this story includes dark, graphic and explicit content matter that is not suitable for readers under the age of 18—or for readers who are uncomfortable with the following subject matter: explicit sex, mentions of sexual abuse, and graphic depictions of violence.

"You're going to die," my sister Briar tells me around a yawn while tucked beneath her embroidered blankets. "I saw it in a dream. You die. But everyone thinks you're me—hey! Why did you stop?" She tilts her blond head toward me expectantly.

I'm holding her brush. It's heavy and silver, so different from the cheap, wooden comb I use. Jealousy is a constant itch I have to smother. It's like Mother says: *Briar may have more material things, but things aren't everything. You have gifts too, Ellen, my Rose.*

My "gifts" aren't as obvious as the shelves of dolls and finery lining the walls of Briar's massive bedroom. Pink walls and buttery-soft carpet form a suite ten times as big as my room downstairs. Her bed alone is big enough for the two of us to lie outstretched on the center of it beneath a lacy canopy.

"Ellen?" Briar tugs on my arm. "Keep going."

Swallowing hard, I finger one of her golden curls and then ease the tangles from it. "No one would ever think I'm you," I reply, knowing exactly what she wants me to say.

"Of course." She giggles, wiggling her nose. "Because I'm prettier." And she is. Just nine years old—two years older than I am—and she already looks more like our mother than I could ever dream to. At least until, her pretty smile fades. "But everyone still likes you more."

"Nuh uh." My stomach drops. I hate when Briar gets this way, like when we play board games and I make the mistake of winning too many times. Everything becomes a contest.

And I always have to lose.

"You're so much better than me," I insist. "I have to be nice. That's all."

Because I'm not like her—not an heiress. If I pout, or scream, or throw a tantrum, I'll be punished and Mother won't be able to see me. Even the thought of it makes my heart ache, and I maneuver the brush more gently through Briar's curls. "Everyone loves *you*."

Her pink lips quirk into a lovely smile, and she shrugs me off to sit back against a wall of pillows. "I know that," she insists. "Even Robert is nicer to you though."

Robert. Her older brother who visits the manor sometimes. He's back now. Occasionally, I pass him in the hallway. Would I say he's nice to me? Maybe. But sometimes I think he looks at me the way Briar does her dolls once they're broken. Like I'm tiny, and plastic, and hollow.

"Ugh." Briar rolls her eyes. "Speak of the devil."

My cheeks grow hot. We aren't allowed to talk like that, not that it matters. Mother isn't the figure standing in the doorway, and Robert doesn't seem to care. Only Briar would ever dare call him unholy anyway; he looks like an angel. His hair is a brighter gold than his sister's, his eyes a deep shade of brown.

"It's late," he says, running his fingers along the collar of a pressed suit. He looks grown up wearing it. Like Briar's father, the master of the house, does. Like a businessman. "Shouldn't you be in bed? *Both* of you?" His eyes cut in my direction.

I cringe, jumping to my feet. "S-sorry—"

"She was getting me a glass of milk," Briar says over me. "That's why she's here. Don't you dare tell."

"It's dangerous to sneak around at night," Robert says, his voice soft. "Don't you know that's when the monsters come out?"

"There's no such thing as monsters," Briar declares, squaring her jaw.

But she's wrong. Monsters live right here in the manor. Sometimes I hear them if I stay up too late: faint scuffling noises from down below… Screaming.

It's why I'm never supposed to leave my room at night. Mother makes me promise I won't—but Briar is the only one worth breaking that promise for.

"Fine, then. If you insist on being a lazy brat, come, Elle." Robert waves his hand, summoning me closer. "I'll go with you."

A part of me wants to stay here with Briar—hide *behind* her if I have to. But Robert is sixteen, practically an adult. I have no choice but to shuffle after him into the hall.

Briar has a whole wing to herself. Even the walls are decorated in soft shades of pink to match the cream carpeted floors. We pass her playroom and the closet where she keeps her winter clothes. There's a servant's stairway back here too. Accompanied by the regal boy beside me, I notice all the flaws here that aren't visible in the grand hallway his family uses. The walls are painted white with cracks in the corners that draw his gaze.

"The kitchens are this way," I gather up the nerve to point toward a door at the base of the steps.

Robert shoots me an odd look. "I know. Your room is down here, isn't it?"

I force myself to nod, my eyes wide. I don't think I've ever seen him in this part of the house before.

Chuckling, Robert nudges my chin with the tips of his fingers and I shiver. He's smiling, one of the few times I've ever seen him do so. "Don't look so surprised," he gently scolds. "You aren't like Briar, are you? You don't act like a child. How old are you?"

Something squirms in my belly as I say, "S-seven."

"Seven." He nods like I've shared some powerful secret. "You seem older sometimes. Older than my sister, anyway."

I look over my shoulder just in case Briar snuck out of her room after us. My heart is pounding harder. My toes curl against the carpet, slick with sweat.

"That's a good thing," he insists. "You aren't naïve like her."

My tongue struggles to copy the strange word. "N-naï—"

"Silly," he says sternly. He leans down, bringing his face close to mine. "You aren't silly. I think you know what a real monster is. Don't you?"

I shake my head.

"Don't lie." Robert brushes my cheek again, forcing me to face him. "Tell me."

All the things Mother always warned me about gnaw at the back of my mind. *Never stay out late. Never come upstairs without permission.* She never told me not to talk to Robert, but...

"Sometimes I hear noises at night," I admit.

When he cocks his head, I realize I was whispering.

"What kind of noises?" he prods, his voice louder than mine.

"Shouting. Yelling. Screaming—"

"Shh!"

I jump as Robert presses his thumb against my lips. Noise echoes at the top of the staircase. Someone's coming.

Before they appear, Robert grabs my arm and steers me into the kitchen. "Here." Upon letting me go, the older boy rummages through a cupboard for a glass and fills it with water from the tap. When he hands it to me, I frown in confusion.

"I think she wanted milk—"

"Wait."

I stiffen at his playful tone, alarmed when he draws the cup beyond my reach. Robert is too serious for games. He doesn't even like to play checkers with Briar. He must be mocking me. Though why?

"You're smarter than Briar," he declares. "Aren't you?"

"I-I—"

"I'm going to show you a real monster," he says over me, leaning in close. "They aren't like they seem in fairytales. Are you brave enough?" He grabs my arm before I can decide and presses the cup of water against my palm, forcing me to take it. "Come on."

He leads me past the kitchen and down a narrow hallway, but my steps falter over the icy concrete floor. I'm not allowed this far, this deep into the basement. My stomach starts to hurt, like it does when Briar makes me bend the rules—such as staying in her room too late. If someone catches me, I might never be allowed upstairs again.

"In here."

Up ahead, Robert stops beside a door. Another man is already standing there and my heart sinks.

"Relax," Robert says, dragging me closer. He eyes the man, his head held high. "You won't tell anyone we were here." His voice rings with authority and the man nods. Then he opens the door and nudges me closer, his hand on my shoulder. "Look…"

My heart pounds as my eyes adjust to the darkness. Monsters have teeth and sharp claws. They thrive in the dark. They growl and prowl and…

They aren't small. Monsters aren't supposed to be hunched on the floor, with delicate limbs and pale skin.

I always thought Briar was the prettiest person I've ever seen, but the girl huddled in a dark room is beautiful. Long, dark hair falls over her like a cape, obscuring most of her tattered, gray shirt and jeans. She's young, maybe even the same age as Robert.

"Go on," Robert goads, pushing me closer.

My hand trembles and most of the water in the cup has spilled down the front of my nightgown by the time I reach her. Her face is bruised, and shiny ropes are wrapped around her arms—like the kind used to tie up the Rottweilers Briar's father owns: chains.

"Closer," Robert insists.

I have no choice but to take another step. Then another…

I jump as the girl lifts her head, her eyes huge in the darkness. "What's your name?" Her voice is so soft that I barely hear her.

"Don't answer," Robert snaps, but it's too late.

My lips are already moving. "E-Ellen," I croak.

The girl smiles. "My…my name is Anna-Natalia." She stares past me to Robert, meeting his gaze directly. But she doesn't tremble like everyone else does around the Winthorp heirs. She doesn't even flinch. "My *name* is Anna-Natalia."

"Go back upstairs, Elle," Robert says, shoving me toward the door. "Now, you know what real monsters look like. They look just like us."

Turning on my heel, I run, escaping the basement and sprinting back upstairs. I return to Briar's room panting, and she observes me from her bed, pouting.

"Where's my milk?"

I can't even speak. Instead, I grab the brush from the edge of her mattress and return it to her vanity. "I should go. Goodnight—"

"Stay with me tonight." She reaches out, and I marvel at her slim fingers. They look just like mine but softer. Cleaner. *Prettier,* like she said. "I don't want to be alone."

"But…" My eyes dart toward her bedroom door. I want to run to my room and crawl beneath my plain covers. I want to forget what Robert showed me. "If anyone else catches me—"

"They won't," Briar insists. "Come!" She pats the space beside her, and I reluctantly crawl onto the mattress, slipping beneath her silk sheets. "You see?" She runs her fingers along my stomach, tickling me. "We're just like real sisters."

"Real sisters," I echo, snuggling as close to her as I dare. Sometimes I forget that's exactly what we are: sisters.

"Ellen?" she whispers.

"Yes?"

"If monsters did really come for me… If I were going to die, you wouldn't let it happen. Would you?"

"No." I shake my head, my heart swelling with protectiveness. "I'd fight them for you. Always."

"Good." She closes her eyes and gestures for me to switch the light off. "Night."

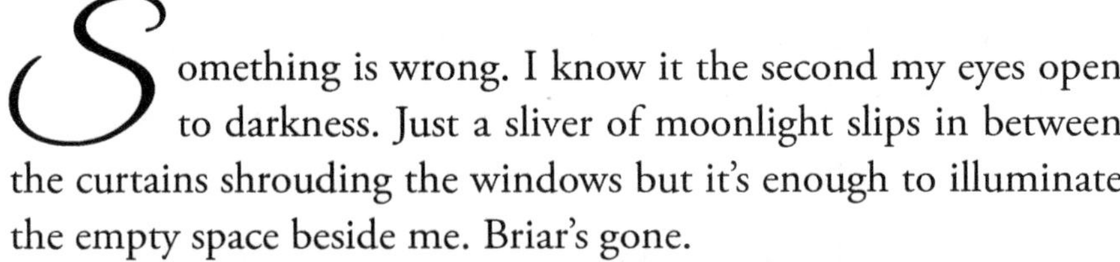

Something is wrong. I know it the second my eyes open to darkness. Just a sliver of moonlight slips in between the curtains shrouding the windows but it's enough to illuminate the empty space beside me. Briar's gone.

As soon as I register that fact I catch a shadow drifting across the wall, ghosting over a shelf of porcelain dolls. Briar? No. It's too massive and terror descends like ice water. This figure is bulky. Someone big. Too big to be Mother or one of the servants.

Too big to be Robert.

Their footsteps are heavy. Cautious. Paralyzed by fear, I crane my neck and find a figure hunched over the foot of the bed. The monster Briar feared. Just as Robert taught me, he looks *human.*

Blond hair peeks from the edges of a black woolen cap. That color makes my heart stop—he's wearing it from head to toe. Black slacks and a dark sweatshirt meant to disguise him in the shadows.

The second he meets my gaze, I know. He's dangerous, just like the men my mother warned me about. What he's holding proves it: something silver glinting in the dark, a forbidden object I'm not allowed to touch.

A knife.

He points it at me, his jaw clenched. "Get up. I said get up," he hisses. His voice sounds strange, with emphasis placed on odd syllables. "Now!" He adjusts the knife, but his hand wavers. His eyes are too wide. Fearful?

Suddenly, he stiffens, his head cocked. Behind him, the door is partially opened, and he cuts his gaze to it. When he turns back to me, he points the knife again, jabbing the edge toward the bed.

"Get under it," he commands. "Now! Don't think. Don't move. Just breathe. You hear me? All you do is fucking *breathe.*"

CHAPTER 1

Noise…
Chaos…
Briar…

The first thing I'm aware of is that I'm blindfolded—a fact that could be a blessing in disguise as my thoughts blur and jumble together. Only one coherent question escapes the fray: *Where am I?*

No answer comes to me immediately. My straining ears can make out only a few words muttered nearby in unfamiliar voices. Deep, *masculine* voices.

Various smells irritate my nostrils as well: sweat, body odor, male. *All* male. God, *where am I?*

I try flexing my shoulders only to wince. My hands are impossible to move, tied behind my back with something rough. Rope?

Oh, God.

Familiar terror gnaws at my belly as moisture gathers in my armpits and sweeps across my palms. At least, now, I have an inkling of my fate. I'm trapped in another one of his games. My nostrils flare with renewed purpose: seeking out *his* scent.

He must have hired lackeys this time; foreign body odor drowns out the stench of his cologne. I can't smell him.

But you can survive this. I fall back on the mantra that has gotten me through every day for sixteen years. *You can survive, Ellen. Focus, Ellen. Breathe, Ellen.*

Ten hours—that's how long I endured last time. My resolve had nearly splintered by the end. I'd almost given in. Almost.

But even psychological wounds eventually heal and leave tougher scar tissue behind. I can last another ten hours with Robert. My brain makes that distinction as the barrage of scents dissipates, revealing one that overpowers the rest: a man's. I taste the nuances in his stench rather than smell them—he's *that* potent, composed of a multitude of different things.

Cigar smoke.

Vodka.

One scent in particular makes my heart stop. Salty and sweet, it's almost as familiar as the flowery perfume wafting from my skin now. *Blood?*

Robert never smokes. He doesn't drink. Whenever he hurts me, he always washes his hands before and after. It is our routine, and he is nothing if not predictable.

No. This is someone new. Someone taller, whose shadow completely blots out what little detail plays across my blindfold. His footsteps are steady. Heavy.

"This her?"

I sense the outline of his fingers before the callused edge of one grazes my forehead.

"You made sure?"

His voice is deep. Almost *too* deep to be intelligible: a series of grated, rumbling notes. There's an accent tucked among them—something thick. Eastern European? Briar had a maid from there once. Sonja.

Sonja liked to read Jane Eyre. She liked scribbling love notes to Robert Sr.'s men before fucking them in the broom closet late at night when she thought no one was looking. Sonja liked a lot of things before Robert took a liking to her.

But another figure from my memory possessed this accent as well. Even though his words were hissed in a whisper, I still remember. *Breathe!*

"Bring her."

Those two words snap me back to the present. Unfamiliar hands grab my shoulders, cinching the soft silk of my blouse. *Briar's* blouse. She dressed me in it lovingly, remarking on how the color complemented my eyes. Our eyes, the same shade of light blue.

"Move!"

A tug on my shoulders hauls me upright and unseen hands shove me forward. Every sound echoes. Four footsteps, including mine. The biggest man takes the lead, I suspect, his gait rhythmic against creaking floorboards.

In contrast, the men holding me dig their nails into my skin and scurry toward an unknown destination. A rusty squeal seconds later conjures the image of an old door opening, and the footsteps trail off.

"Move!"

Something rams into my side and I stagger for balance until my cheek strikes a hard surface. It's warm. *Human.*

"Get her on the bed."

Those harsh hands return to my shoulders to fulfill the command.

"Sit her on the edge…like that. Cut her hands free."

A metallic hiss sends a shiver down my spine—then *pain!* Fire courses through my fingertips as circulation returns to them. I long to flex each one, but I know better. Instead, I keep them close, settling them onto my lap.

These men kept my skirt on, at least. Her skirt. The hem comes down past my knees, and I've never been so grateful for four inches of satin. It will buy me more time.

Ten hours. I've already lasted ten minutes. *You can do this,* the courageous part of my soul whispers. But then that voice dies in the wake of two more words uttered in that guttural cadence.

"Leave us."

The two smaller men scatter in the direction we entered—but it's all wrong. No. No. I don't smell Robert, and he'd never leave me alone with another man. Not his lackey. Not even his own father.

Most alarming of all, this man certainly is no Winthorp. His voice isn't familiar and this house doesn't smell like any property on the familial grounds.

They took me from the motorcade…

Fire sears through my skull as memories return in snatches. The clearest one is of her face. *Briar.* So beautiful, dominated by that pure, sweet smile. "I want you there," she insisted. "We're sisters, after all."

Sisters. I cherished how that word sounded in her soft cadence, tucking that moment inside myself like one of the trinkets hidden in my secret cache. Love was more precious than a button or rock I'd stolen away. Those four words meant everything. *I want you there.*

But the memory of that moment serves as a weak antidote to the terror paralyzing me now. More bits and pieces come back.

I was in the car—the beautiful limousine for once, instead of one of the servant vans that took up the rear. For part of the way, I was even sitting beside her while she braided my hair. "We look alike now," she wistfully remarked, beaming at our reflections in the polished windows.

We look alike. The phrase haunts me. As if I could ever look like Briar, with her lighter ringlets and her creamy skin. The only feature we truly share is our eyes. Our mother's eyes. Large, round, and blue. In every other respect, she takes after her father, with a beautiful aristocratic nose and a graceful neck. Every

Winthorp possesses the same subtle characteristics—markings of the blood, they like to claim. Good blood. Blue blood.

I take after my father, whoever he is.

Briar loves to tout our tentative resemblance anyway—especially to her benefit. *I* am the one the maid saw sneaking out back two summers ago. *I* am the one who scurried out of the room of that visiting businessman one winter.

And now…

We look alike.

"Take off the blindfold." That voice…

I swallow hard, uneasy. Robert has found a new monster to play with. Someone who shares his flair for the dramatic. *But where is he?* My tormentor always relishes this part of the game. How he enjoys savoring my fear as I try to piece together where I am. Admittedly, it wasn't this hard before; he never strays too far from the property.

His favorite lairs are the boathouse, or the deserted crypt, or the east wing. I could always hear the bluebirds chirping throughout the grounds, no matter which corner of the estate he deemed my chosen cell.

My ears strain, searching for that faint, familiar song. This time of year, they're nearly deafening, able to be heard in even the farthest reaches of Winthorp Manor.

Two seconds. Three.

I hear nothing.

"Take off the blindfold."

The harsh rasp of syllables steals my breath away. I know anger on Robert. On Robert Sr. Even on Briar. They stutter. They shout. They scream.

None of them ever exude their impatience to the point where I can sense it in the air. Or taste it: copper on my tongue. This man isn't a Winthorp.

The realization coaxes my body into action. My sore fingers finally contort, trembling after what must have been hours of captivity. Whoever tied my blindfold snagged bits of my hair in the process and every tug on the knot at the base of my neck rips tiny strands loose from my scalp—comparable to my pathetic hopes being ripped from underneath me one by one.

I don't hear the bluebirds.

I can't smell Robert's favorite cologne.

When I finally get the knot loosened enough to uncover my eyes…

I see hell.

Mother used to say it was beautiful, forsaking the teachings of the local priest. "Hell is a rose," she used to murmur, her gaze turned inward, wistful and distant. "A flawless one, with all the life sucked out of it. The thorns have become knives. Its leaves have swallowed up the stalk. It's grotesque. It's deadly. But never forget that, underneath the violence, it's still beautiful."

He is beautiful. Or he was once. Blond hair draws my attention first—a sun-kissed gold in places, darkened with age in others. It's been clawed back from his face into a ponytail longer than mine was before Briar trimmed it. His eyes are that dangerous color between blood and brown. Like a flame, they catch the light filtering in through a sloppily boarded-up window beside him. His face is angular. Chiseled. Stone. Every feature is sculpted to convey just one emotion: determination. The way an owl might watch the mice scurrying underfoot in the stables. Or the way Robert used to look at me.

The way the devil looks, I presume, as if he has all the time in the world. More than ten hours.

An eternity to torture me.

CHAPTER 2

"Say your name." As the stranger issues the command, he lowers his eyes to fully take me in, and the coldness in them unsettles my every nerve. "Your name."

It should be a simple question with an even simpler answer. I'm Ellen. Just Ellen. I work as a maid in the Winthorp household—on paper. But papers can be forged, identities erased. Or mistaken.

I can't get Briar's last words to me out of my head: *We look alike.*

Wherever I am, I don't think she's here with me. This room must have been a bedroom once. Behind the man stands a rickety dresser, lopsided with age and disuse. Hanging on the wall above it is a mirror caked with dust. Only the hint of my reflection is visible, but the woman staring back at me is a stranger. Her brown hair is neatly coifed, half coiled into a braid and the rest cascading down her shoulders. Her blouse is silk, and—though it isn't visible from this angle—her burgundy skirt is satin. Her shoes are worth more than a Winthorp servant earns in a year. Her lips are a soft shade of pink.

"We look alike," Briar told me shortly before leaving the limo and taking another car to the airport. "I need to make a detour," she said. "We'll meet up later. I'm going to make sure you have the best time in London! You'll see."

Only London has never felt farther away. My chest has never felt so tight. This room is airless—I'm suffocating. For all her indifference to me, Briar has never played along in one of Robert's games before.

"I won't ask you again, Little One." The man strokes fingers caked with mud across my cheek, and I flinch. There's no gentleness in his touch. No malice, either. "Say your name."

"My name is…" My voice fails me as my gaze returns to the mirror and I finally identify the woman staring back at me. "My name is Briar Winthorp."

The man doesn't laugh at the admission. He doesn't squint as if to make out the pauper hiding behind these fancy clothes. He nods once, his eyes narrowing. "Your father has enemies, Little One."

I inhale sharply as more memories trickle back.

I was in the motorcade…

"I have to run an errand," Briar said. She left, only the procession continued as if she were still there beside me. The security remained, as did the four-man bodyguard detail lurking on either side of the main procession.

We look alike.

"Look at me," the stranger snaps, demanding my attention once more. He's closer now, but I still have to strain to take him in fully. He's tall, taller than Robert. Gray fatigues and a dark jacket shroud most of his frame. Muscle shapes him down to his massive hands. He cracks the knuckles on each finger one by one, aware of me watching. He's no businessman from the Winthorp industries. No, he's something else, a title that takes my brain nearly a minute to define. *Soldier. Mercenary. Murderer.*

"Your fiancé as well," he continues. "He has enemies. Can you tell me why that may be?"

Fiancé? He must mean Daniel. *Briar's* fiancé, a man who, to his own merit, has amassed a power almost comparable to Robert Winthorp Sr.'s.

"Answer me, Little One." The stranger strokes my hair this time, snagging loose strands as he does.

Robert used to touch me the same way—back when he still relished the thrill of hunting me down like cattle. Lately, he's been lazier in his endeavors, cornering me without even half the cunning he once employed. But that brief respite has made me weak against this method.

It's remarkable how much can be conveyed through someone's fingertips. Robert's are soft and maliciously manicured, and they bruised when he struck me too hard. *This* man's skin is callused and rough. From work. From brutality. From abuse. Scars mark him down to the base of his wrists, like the kind Briar disguises with long sleeves and silk blouses.

"I will warn you now." The stroking touch becomes a manacle of fingers latching onto my skull and forcing my chin upright. "Speak. Obey."

"He…he's a businessman, Daniel is," I stammer as his thumb grazes my lower lip, capturing each word.

"A businessman?" The stranger laughs. "That is one way to put it, Little One."

One way to put it. Criminal is another—a word only the most brazen of journalists dare to use in their headlines.

"What…what are you going to do to me?" I croak.

"Do to you?" His gaze roves downward, settling over the high neckline of Briar's blouse. Once again, he resembles Robert.

I know that look. *You can survive ten hours,* a part of me whispers. But it's cold comfort—this time, I'm lying.

"I am going to punish you, Little One," the man tells me, his tone a grating hiss. "Your father. Your lover. They took something from me."

Without warning, I'm shoved backward, my fall broken by the rickety mattress.

"I will take something from them."

The soles of his boots strike the floor in tandem. Closer. Closer. I can't make his expression out from this angle—just a circle of blackness where his face should be. His body doesn't disguise his intentions, however. His hands move to his belt. Leather kisses leather with a telltale hiss, followed by the hum of a zipper being undone.

Zzrrrippp…

I've heard that sound a million times before, yet it never ceases to steal my breath away.

"You will suffer," the man tells me, deftly undoing the front of his slacks, revealing a sliver of gray boxers underneath. "Unless…" He pauses, hovering on the edge of a question. Something vital. My answer will determine the next phase of this nightmare. "Unless you tell me what I need to know."

I nod. It's instinctive: a desperate jerking of my chin even though I know that salvation is a lie. I'm stalling, and he's merely prolonging this part of the game. Robert's decided to use a stand-in tonight—that has to be it. Cuckholding me wouldn't be the worst thing he's ever done.

I can survive. I can…

"Answer me, Little One. Believe me when I say that I do not want to hurt you." The stranger's voice deepens on the edge of a dangerous note. It's soft, almost like a whisper. Like a plea: *Don't fuck with me.* "Where is your father running to?"

My father? Oh. I blink, fighting to remember. Briar's father. Where is he running?

"I-I…"

Wait. Robert wouldn't write this script. There's no begging. No salacious words he likes to force me to say. No stripping me bare to give me a "taste" of what being his favorite saves me from.

And never, ever did he mention Robert Sr.

I read once that fear of a name only increases fear of the thing itself. In that case, the mere mention of his father must terrify Robert. He even avoids being called his full name. *Bobby,* he prefers his minions to whimper.

"I-I…"

"You do not have long to answer." The stranger cocks his head as if catching wind of a far-off noise. A slow smile shapes his mouth, chilling me to my very core. The hands at his waistband shift, and every deliberate movement makes my chest feel tighter, my heart beat faster.

"I don't know," I insist. "I…I don't know what you mean—"

Too late. The rotting floorboards broadcast his advance. My throat is too dry—I can't speak. I can't scream. I can only watch his hand descend before it snatches at the hem of Briar's skirt. The garment was made especially for her from a designer in France—and he tears it right down the middle.

Weak, I flex my fingers at my sides. Not to cover myself, but to brace. Towering above me on a mass of sculpted muscle, this man will crush me. Experience warns me to arch my back as much as I dare, giving my lungs enough leverage to fill before he does.

Instead… The brunt of his palm grazes my upper thigh and my thoughts dissipate. Ice shoots through my veins, rendering me frozen. It's not his touch that alarms me. It's his expression. There's no lust. No fire. No thrill at the game.

Just anger smoldering in the thumb he draws across my right knee.

To tease?

No. To *feel*: the ropey length of a scar. One of the many Robert left behind.

My neck aches as I crane it in order to watch in horror as his touch continues to roam. He rakes his hands over them all. The cuts. The bruises. Some healed. Some not. He takes one of his fingers, long and callused, and traces a fresher cut along my hip.

My belly roils at the slow, deliberate appraisal, and I can't swallow a gasp. Robert gropes me. He…studies me?

When I look up at his face, I'm forced to reckon with the realization laid bare over the harsh features. Within an instant, the hard veneer of a soldier is stripped away, revealing something much more terrifying: disgust. Then rage.

Tilting his head back, he seeks my gaze out and devours me whole. "Who the hell are you?"

CHAPTER 3

Run! It's a new impulse, something I've never felt around Robert. He'd never let me escape, but this man…

He waits until I've rolled onto my side, flailing for the edge of the mattress, before he lunges, seizing a handful of my hair. One hard yank rips me from the bed, forcing me to my knees. I land hard, tasting blood but too stunned to scream.

"Who?"

The grated question rings out unanswered. With a hiss of irritation, he finds the truth himself by bunching the sleeves of my blouse and pulling. His first attempt knocks me forward and only my palms save my face from a nasty meeting with the floor. His second yank strips me bare. I'm not wearing a bra and instinct drives me to hunch over, which displays my back to the creature pacing behind me.

My face may have fooled him, but my body does not. Years of abuse betray me. Hissing his rage, the soldier is forced to admit the ruse.

"Fuck. Vanya!" The door opens seconds later and two men race inside, stopping just short of where I'm kneeling.

"Look," their leader commands, his tone casual. As if this really were a game. Hide-and-seek, maybe? Only he's lost the round. "Does she look like an heiress to you?"

Air lashes my back as he moves. Seconds later, his fingers are in my hair and he tugs my head back, forcing my gaze to the ceiling. My eyelids flutter, shrouding the shape of him hovering on the outskirts of my vision.

"Her face is convincing," he declares begrudgingly. "But this bitch is no Winthorp. I know the mark of Robert's whores when I see them. She was a decoy."

He shoves me aside and I wind up facedown, tasting dust. *This bitch is no Winthorp.* Some small part of me snickers at that. It's like knowing a secret no one gives a damn about. A tiny, little detail that makes his statement a lie.

Not that it matters.

"Get out." He's not talking to me. No… This man and I are not through with our game.

His boot strikes my hip, knocking me onto my side. Blurred vision gives me a few seconds of reprieve. And even though I can't see his face, my imagination has no trouble conjuring an expression to match his coarse tone.

Eyes like fire and a fearsome scowl.

"I would have shown mercy to Briar," he admits while his shadow looms above, lacking all definition. "She did not ask for this. But you…"

He stoops to clutch my shoulders and drag me up to his level. I taste vodka on his breath, which perfumes the air as his features come back into focus.

"*You.* How much money did he offer you, hmm? What was your soul worth?"

My soul? Sluggishly, my brain pieces together what he means. Bought. He thinks Robert Sr. bought me to be his daughter's double. He thinks the man would be that kind. That generous.

The truth is much crueler. You don't buy a sacrifice.

"Whatever it was," the man continues, "I hope every penny was worth the pain you will suffer in her place." His nails graze my skull as he lets me go and stands. "Tell me what you know and I'll consider making your death quick."

"N-nothing." The truth spills out of me in a broken whisper. Nothing. I know nothing.

"We look alike," Briar told me. That was all. "Like sisters…"

I'm so lost in the memory that I don't register him moving until it's too late. Brutal fingers circle my throat and clench. Like a rag doll, I'm wrenched to my feet. Shoved back. I fall. Hit something soft…

And then unmovable steel pins me down. He's more than heavy. He's a battering ram, crushing me to the mattress. What little air I suck into my lungs has no escape and forms a plug at the base of my throat.

He squeezes until stars appear, dancing through the air and obscuring his face. His *face*. For some reason, I force my burning eyes to refocus, seeking out as much detail of it as I can. I always thought Robert would be the one to kill me. Not a stranger, his gaze like midnight.

I'm dying. I feel it—my limbs jerk, controlled by instinct. Blood surges to my head. My pulse hammers against my eardrums. Right as my vision begins to fade, the pressure loosens a fraction. Just enough for me to suck in air again.

"I've been patient, Little One," he murmurs as I sputter. "Perhaps you need more incentive?"

My breast. He cups it, capturing the flesh against his palm, grazing my nipple. There's no ownership, like how Robert likes to caress me. Just rough, slow possession. I feel his nails, pinching and sharp.

"I will give you one more chance to tell me what you know," he says. "All of it."

He has no idea how dangerous a question he's proposed. What I know? Nothing. If anything, he's supplying more answers than I could ever deduce on my own. What was the word he used? A decoy.

We look alike.

"Robert knew I was coming for him," the man growls, flexing his grip until I gasp. "You will tell me how."

Nothing. I can't speak as terror crashes through my entire being. Even Robert couldn't reduce me to this state so quickly. My eyes prickle in warning before heat spills from them.

"I. Don't. Know."

He frowns at the pathetic syllables I manage to muster. With a shift of his weight, he mounts me fully, wedging his bulk in the narrow gap between my thighs. My feeble attempts to resist him are defeated by his knee. He uses it as a battering ram to gain enough leverage to draw his pelvis in close.

No man but Robert has *ever* been this close—and this newer creature is bigger. Crueler. Rougher.

"How?" The man recaptures my throat, caressing my windpipe. "How did he know, hmm? We were careful. Does he have a spy? An informant?"

My answering wheeze draws a chilling response: he sighs.

"Please do not test me, Little One." His touch leaves my breast and slides between my legs.

"N-no!" My hands hammer against unyielding muscle even though it's in vain.

I learned a long time ago that it's futile to resist. Admittedly, I've gotten better at it. Robert used to savor this reaction in me. He would ease a finger inside to prepare me for fucking.

This man…

He shoves me down, rearing back on his braced knee. "How many of my men do you think you can handle, Little One? Should I go first?"

The threat is real. His eyes reveal nothing but endless darkness. He'd do it.

I feel the evidence for myself, hard against my hip.

"How did he know?" He trails his fingers from my throat to my chin, cupping it so that I'm forced to meet his gaze directly. In it,

I find only darkness. "Tell me and I won't touch you. I swear on your life."

But I have no answer to give him. No way to save myself.

"Your choice." The man's nostrils flare. Then, without warning, he climbs off the bed and redoes the zipper of his pants.

I can't help the frantic way my chest heaves, desperately seeking air. The places where he touched me burn as if scorched. I don't know if it's a trick of the light or if the dark strands of hair wrapped around his fingers really are mine, torn from my scalp. Still, I don't move. I lie there, at his mercy.

I seal my fate.

CHAPTER 4

"I hope you are just foolish," the man laments, sounding almost genuine. "Because bravery won't serve you here."

He turns his back to me, adjusting his clothing with sharp, curt tugs on the fabric. Only from this angle do I catch the scars that riddle the base of his throat. Long, jagged, barely concealed by the fall of his hair.

As if sensing my reaction, he faces me again, giving my body a chilling appraisal. "I'm sure you've heard the rumors. What happens to those who cross me." He waits as if for me to confess.

But I wasn't lying. I know nothing, especially not of him.

"Fine. Perhaps not a fool, but reckless?" he wonders, shrugging. "If you won't talk, then you will serve another purpose."

He returns to my end of the bed and snatches my wrist. Pain sears through my arm as he drags me after him. I stagger, flailing for balance while the room blurs around me. He takes me into the hall and down a short flight of stairs. When we reach the bottom, I rush to piece together our newer surroundings. The smells register first.

Men. A lot of them. Their overwhelming stench chokes me, and I remember his threat. His promise. *How many do you think you can handle?*

It's darker here. The only light sneaks in through boarded-up windows. In the resulting shadow, I make out featureless faces. Shapes. At least ten figures are crowding this room, maybe twenty. All are suspiciously silent apart from a few laughs as I stagger in their leader's wake. There's an animal here as well. It growls as we come too close. A dog?

A large one, I realize, as I spot it crouched in a metal cage in a back corner. Without a word, the leader hauls me to it and undoes the latch with his free hand.

"Get!" he commands the beast, who skulks off, brushing my knee on its way past.

Before the animal has fully left the cage, I'm shoved in its place, forced onto my hands and knees to fit inside the enclosure. Metal clangs as the door is slammed and the latch engaged.

"Enjoy your new pet," the man announces before leaving the room. "But no one touch her. *Yet.*"

I've been a bone before: an object placed on display to be watched. Guarded. Coveted.

These men don't whistle and howl like Robert's. Even the dog does nothing more than sniff me. In the darkness, I sense a few searing gazes directed my way, but they're silent for the most part, focused on whatever task is occupying them.

We must be in a house of some kind. An old one. This narrow room with its faded wallpaper and sloped floors might have been a drawing room at one point, envisioned to entertain visitors or gatherings.

Now? Its purpose appears more nefarious. There are boxes dispersed in between the men. What they contain, I can't tell, but scents irritate my nostrils beneath the overwhelming stench of sweat. Chemical in nature. Gunpowder?

But when one of the men nearest my cage stands, hefting an object beside him, I realize they're all armed—with more than the small pistols Robert and his men carry. Long guns. Big guns. They prop them along the walls, always within reach.

This space must be a storeroom of some kind, containing materials that need fifteen pairs of watchful eyes to guard them at all times. Five men are sitting at a card table in the center of the room, conversing in snippets of a language I can't make out. Five more have taken various positions against the walls, while the rest are scattered in between, focused on packing something into the boxes. Something small. Round?

"Uh-huh!"

An object slams against the top of my cage. A hand? It belongs to a man who appears grotesque in the darkness. His eyes are the only feature I can clearly make out. They're narrowed, focused on my face.

"No peeking," he barks in accented English. "You want to keep that face pretty? Look at the wall."

I obey. The wallpaper in this corner is peeling in places, revealing dried, decaying wood underneath. As strange as it feels to admit, it's a slightly better view than what I'm used to. Ironic, considering that Robert's room is grand, as is the one he makes me sleep in. The walls are painted white. The floors are polished hardwood. Everything down to the bedsheets is of the finest quality. And every second I spent trapped within those four walls, I feared I might go blind.

I wished I would.

Darkness obscures the horror of my current surroundings. At the same time, it compounds it. There's nothing to distract me from my own thoughts and what they imply. Briar, beautiful Briar. Did she know all along what trap she was leading me into?

My eyes sting, and blinking doesn't keep the tears at bay. They spill, hot and burning down my cheeks. For the first time in ages, my initial impulse isn't to wipe them away. I let them fall and relish the bitter fear that leaves me trembling.

Fear. It's funny how such a terrible, awful emotion can be welcome. I once thought Robert had driven all emotion out of me—but he hasn't. I don't want to die here.

"Relax."

My cage is slapped again from above, this time decidedly more softly. The blow draws me farther back against the bars with my knees pulled up to shield as much of myself as I can.

"You don't have to fear rape," the man hisses. There's a roughness in his voice but no mocking. He's not lying. "Mischa can be cruel, but he never lets his men go that far."

The man jerks his chin toward the rest of the room as if to say, *See? Look.*

I sneak a glimpse from the corner of my eye, surprised by what I find. Minutes after my arrival and I still haven't drawn any more attention than a few guarded looks. Not out of respect, I suspect. More like...*disinterest?* Almost as if so many women have been locked within this cage that the novelty has worn off.

"You don't have that to fear from him. He is insane," the man beside the cage admits, "but not a monster. He will hurt you, though, if you do not give him what he wants. Do *not* make him angry." He stresses every word and taps the bars for emphasis. "He won't fuck you, but he'll still hit you."

My arm stings in memory. Oddly enough, I can't decide what I fear more: sexual violence or brutality? I've never had a choice between the two before.

"You want to ask something," the man prompts, hissing out the words. "Ask it now. Get it over with. You already know the answer."

"Will...will he kill me?" My voice trickles weakly in the shadow of his.

He's right though. I already know the answer, even before he nods.

"Yes. He will kill you. But, if you obey and keep quiet, he will make it quick. Try to make a scene or challenge him and..." He drags his thumb across his throat. Slowly.

My eyes drift shut as I fight to suck in air. *Keep breathing.* It's the one mantra that can save me when all else fails. *Keep breathing.*

But my ragged breaths are too loud, drowning out the muted noise coming from the rest of the room—and this is the one time when I need to focus. Gathering any and every clue I can is the only hope I have to… *What?* Perhaps just learn the motives of the man who will kill me.

"Y-your name?" I tilt my head back and strain my eyes through the dark, fighting to make out as much of my companion as I can.

He's old. Maybe fifty. The gray speckling his cropped hair catches what few flecks of light enter the room. I can't tell how well questioning him will go over. But I have nothing left to lose.

"What is your name?"

"Ivan." He scoffs. "They call me Vanya. However, it will be better for you not to—"

"M-Mischa?" *That* name tastes strange on my tongue. Two clashing syllables, one soft, the other violent and harsh. "Is that *his* name?"

Vanya scoffs again, shaking his head. The motion alone reveals that he didn't mean to let that detail slip. "I suggest you not use that one, either—" He breaks off suddenly, cocking his head. Then he curses and kicks the side of my cage. "Hush. Keep quiet and look at the wall."

He's gone a heartbeat later, marching toward the center of the room while two sets of footsteps approach from an outside hall. The heaviest pair belongs to *him*. Mischa. I know that even before I hear his voice, lashing like a whip that commands total silence in its wake.

"Out."

The room itself trembles as fifteen men lurch into action like a well-oiled machine. Not all of them leave, however. One set of footsteps lingers behind the rest—they're unsteady, betraying a slight limp on one side. From age or injury? I can't tell.

Apart from him and Mischa, there is one other man. He comes closer to my cage than his leader, his footsteps light and lazy. "Is this the decoy?" he wonders as the back of my neck prickles beneath his unfamiliar gaze. He too has an accent I can't place. "You must be slipping, Mischa. I didn't think even Winthorp could ever fool you—"

"You have a job to do," Mischa warns. "Do it."

"In front of her?" the other man asks.

"She won't live long enough to report anything of use to anyone." There's no malice in the threat. Mischa could be commenting on the weather for all the emotion his voice holds. Death must be that simple to him. That easy. "You have an hour. Vanya will watch you. I shouldn't have to remind you, Xavier, that if you short me, I will kill you."

"I wouldn't dream of deceiving you, *Pakhan*," Xavier simpers, but even I recognize the careful way he melds the taunt with a hint of respect. He knows which lines not to cross.

Apparently, the display satisfies Mischa enough to leave without reinforcing his brutality. In his wake, the air thins. I've been holding my breath all this time.

"Make it quick," Vanya says, apparently taking up the commanding role in his leader's absence.

Despite his warning, I can't resist the temptation to look. A furtive glance over my shoulder reveals that the two men are standing before the card table in the center of the room.

A light has been switched on. The weak glow casts enough illumination to make out the two men's features. One is gnarled, with graying black hair and a scar along his jaw. Vanya. The other is younger. A pair of glasses rests upon his Roman nose, and he's wearing a suit that does its best to convey wealth, but the fit is poor. It's not tailored. *Stolen*, a part of me suspects.

That man places a briefcase upon the table which he opens. Even from this angle, I recognize the stacks of paper contained within. Money. A lot of money.

A memory unfurls from the furthest reach of my consciousness, too quickly to fight. *Cologne. Silk. Copper.* That night Robert came to me, his face bloodied, a stack of bills clutched in his fist.

"Shall we play a game?" he asked, knowing full well that I couldn't refuse. "Tell me." He threw the bloodied cash in my face while I remained seated on the bed. "What is real and what is not?"

I learned a lesson then that remains with me to this day: Nothing is more important to a man than his money. Not women. Not drugs. Not family. Not even his soul.

This Mischa must hoard it at the expense of everything else. By selling something?

As Xavier removes stack after stack of dollars—American from what I can tell—Vanya approaches a cluster of cardboard boxes in one corner of the room. After assessing the cash, he hefts two boxes and brings them closer to the table.

"They're packed," he explains as he sets the second box down. "Ready to ship. You can sell them at the going rate with a little bit of interest for the inconvenience of having to accommodate you directly."

Irritation flits across Xavier's face almost too quickly to catch. "Fine," he says, still removing stack after stack from his briefcase.

As the growing pile continues to climb, I can't help but stare. It's more money than I've ever seen in one place. Even Robert never carries so much on him at one time. The obscene display betrays a more nefarious purpose, however. What on Earth could one box contain to be worth so much?

I shy away from the answer and face the wall. After a few more minutes, Xavier and Vanya seem to conclude their business. The former leaves, his briefcase in tow. I hear it swishing through the air at his side as he turns down that narrow outside hall. When he's gone, Vanya just sighs. There's a leathery hiss like that of paper being sorted, counted, and stored, though I never saw a safe.

Just when I gather up the nerve to peek again, he calls to me. "You'd do best to forget what you saw. If you want to extend your life for however long you can, anyway."

I don't dare turn away again. Instead, I study the wallpaper. The base is dark gray with leaves in a lighter print forming a simple design that crawls out in every which direction. Far, far away to the farthest reaches of the room.

"I have to go," Vanya says after a second's silence. Something unspoken hides within his weary tone. A warning: *Keep to yourself. Stare at the wall.* "When I return…if…I'll bring you something to eat."

But why? My welfare has to be at the bottom of his leader's list. For whatever reason, he made this offer solely out of kindness. Or perhaps pity. One word he used rings ominously. *If.*

If you are still alive.

"Th-thank you," I force myself to whisper regardless.

Without bothering to respond, the man leaves, switching the light off and drenching me in shadow.

CHAPTER 5

I'm alone for barely five minutes before the other men return. With quiet efficiency, they take up their vacated positions, and I'm ignored once again. Heeding Vanya's warning, I don't move from my kneeling position. I stare at the wall and count the seconds. It's a familiar habit, though my surroundings differ from my room in Robert's suite. The basic gist of the game never changes.

Wait for the monster's return. How long will this one take?

Two hours? Four? By the sixth, biological concerns take precedence over psychological ones. My bladder aches, painfully full. Noises rumble from my stomach, clashing with the occasional murmured conversation from the men. The floor of the cage is lined only in crumpled newspaper that chafes against my contorted limbs. Using it for anything but padding is an uncomfortable dilemma to contemplate.

So I stall.

Breathe, Ellen. My lungs expand to obey my old mantra, and for the first time in years, my brain replays snippets of the creature who originally inspired it. Not Robert, though he is similar in shape. A man. A boy. Someone who didn't belong, his eyes catlike in the darkness.

"You breathe," he hissed to me. "You don't think. Don't feel. Just breathe..."

A noise breaks my concentration, dragging me back to the present. Night must have fallen. I can barely see the leaves on the wallpaper anymore when Vanya finally returns. I recognize his unsteady gait even before his hand slams against the top of my cage.

"If I let you out, you obey me. No questions. No complaints. Understand? Try to run and Mischa will be your least concern."

I nod. At the mere hint of freedom, my muscles throb in torment, and I unfurl my sore limbs the moment I hear the latch disengage.

"Slow," Vanya barks as I twist in the narrow space and pull myself through the cage's opening. "Slow...wait—"

I freeze, crouched at his feet while my eyes struggle to adjust to the shadow.

"Here. Put this on."

Something soft brushes my cheek. I reach up, trying to decipher the garment through touch alone. It's thin. Satin? It sports sleeves like a shirt but opens in the center and seems long enough to cover me at least to my knees.

"It's the only thing I could find," Vanya adds almost apologetically. "Hurry up. Then follow me and keep your head down."

He shifts his weight, blocking me from sight—either on purpose or accidentally—as I scramble into what I quickly realize is a robe. After tying the thin sash around my waist, I rise to my feet, forced to cling to the wall for balance. Movement is painful, but I grit my teeth and face Vanya without swaying. He towers above me, almost as tall as his leader. After casting me an appraising glance, he heads for a doorway, leaving me to follow.

Mischa may be the leader here, but I suspect that Vanya isn't too far behind him in their hierarchy. There's respect conveyed in the fact that no one questions him as he leads me from the room and down a narrow hallway.

A bulb hanging from the ceiling illuminates a row of closed doors and more peeling wallpaper. Eventually, Vanya stops beside one door and opens it. "Use it," he says, jerking his chin toward the opening.

A bathroom lurks beyond, small and cramped, but containing a toilet at least and a rusted sink. I nearly collapse with relief, but when I attempt to close the door, Vanya shakes his head.

"Not all the way. I won't look," he adds when I stiffen. "Go on."

My body is in too much distress to give a damn if he does watch. Crouching as low over the toilet as I dare, I relieve myself. As my bladder empties, I have no choice but to face the woman watching me from the dust-covered mirror above the sink. She's pale, her hair hanging wild around her shoulders. A sheer black robe doesn't shield much of her body. Not its nakedness. Not its scars.

"If you're done, hurry up," Vanya warns.

Obediently, I wipe and flush the rickety toilet only to realize that the plumbing must have given out years ago. My waste just sits there, mingling with others I didn't notice in my haste. Vomit surges up my throat, but I manage to choke it down and stagger to the sink to wash my hands. There's soap at least. With my wet fingers, I slick the worst of my tangled curls back before tapping on the door to convey that I'm finished.

When I creep into the hallway, Vanya casts me a single glance before heading farther down the hall. We reach another doorway that opens onto a room that might have been a kitchen once. Now, there's too much clutter to tell. Boxes crowd the few countertops. The stove has been gutted, which leaves an empty space now filled with bags of garbage. The only item in working condition appears to be a stained refrigerator with duct tape on the sides to seal it. Vanya has to try twice to heave it open only to reveal that it contains just a pitcher of water and a loaf of bread.

"Here." He breaks off a slice and hands it to me. After rummaging through the chaos scattered over the counter, he surfaces with a glass and fills it with water.

I accept both, genuinely grateful. "Thank you—"

"Don't thank me," he snaps, jerking his chin toward the food in my hands. "Hurry up and eat."

I devour the bread in three bites and down the water just as quickly. Now that the shock of my predicament has set in, horror and familiarity slowly replace the fear. I've been a prisoner before. I know the role to play. I also know that most captors don't offer their prey a shred of dignity—as much as can be found in a robe and some privacy to use the restroom—or let them from their cell for a walk. Not without a reason.

Why? Guilt? I try to suss out his motives as I gingerly rub my hands together to scrape the crumbs from them. The old man is good at containing his secrets, however. I discern nothing from his stern expression. Just the cold knowledge that, as much as I'm trying to understand him, he's already unraveled me.

"What's your name?" he demands, catching my probing stare.

My heart races at the question. Common sense warns me to lie. But…kindness is such a rare gift, deserving of the same in return. Even Robert hasn't broken me beyond that point.

"My name is—"

"Here you are."

My body reacts to the dangerously soft voice before I turn and see him there, towering in the doorway. Mischa.

Slowly, his eyes flicker from me to Vanya, but the old man doesn't draw half of the rage building in his gaze. "I told you to bring her to *me*," he says. Strained politeness keeps his voice above that unsettling growl.

My brain scrambles to place it. Respect?

"You did," Vanya says, nodding in deference, but there's nothing at all submissive about his posture. He snatches the cup from my grip and refills it with water from the still open fridge. When he places it in my grasp, Mischa's irises darken, honing in on my throat and the black robe drawn tight around me.

"Bring her," he snarls, no longer sounding as composed as he did before. "Now."

"When she finishes," Vanya says calmly. To me, he crooks his fingers in the universal symbol for hurry up.

"Vanya—"

"She'll be better able to withstand your methods on a full stomach, don't you think?" It's not so much a suggestion as it is an insinuation of something.

Whatever it is makes the younger man flinch. "Are you challenging me, Ivan?"

My throat contracts at the lethality of those words. How he says them. *Challenge.* As if it's the ultimate crime.

"No." Beside me, Vanya stiffens, lowering his head. "Of course not, *Pakhan.*"

"Good." Two steps bring Mischa closer. Heavy, wide steps that rattle the peeling tiled floor. "Then she can *finish.*"

It's a dare. One that haunts me as my gaze reconnects with Vanya's. He motions for me to drink and I robotically gulp from the glass. The moment I've drained it, Mischa advances. From the corner of my eye, I see him reach for me, but the ferocity of his grip catches me off guard. I stagger into the counter, knocking an unseen array of objects to the floor. The glass slips from my grasp. Shatters. Something pierces the sole of my right foot in a barrage of searing pain, but I'm dragged forward without mercy. Back down the hallway. Through the room with the cage. Beyond that. Stairs. Hallway. Silence. Room.

Shoved forward, I struggle to make out my surroundings. A bed is paces away, near a rickety dresser positioned by the window. Above, a naked light bulb casts pale light and flickering shadows. Behind me, the door closes.

And my tormentor advances as though he has all the time in the world to play this next phase of the game. Without warning, he runs his hand along my shoulder. His touch burns beneath the thin fabric of the robe and I jump back, preparing to withstand any assault. Anything but the callous swipe that dislodges the garment from behind.

"Have you thought about my offer?" he wonders as I stiffen.

I have: the "truth" in exchange for a quick death. How utterly used to violence he must be to think that those are tempting odds. And, to him, they *are.* There's no mistaking that.

He will kill you quickly, Vanya insisted as if that was somehow the preferable outcome to this nightmare.

Maybe it is.

Rather than speak, I say nothing. It's stifling in this room. The window is nailed shut, preventing any circulation. Sweat springs beneath my armpits and along my neck. He's perspiring as well. The stench of salt seeps from his pores, but it's not potent enough to reek.

I'm too busy trying to place his position that I miss the next move he makes. A shove to my hip nudges me closer to the bed. The mattress brushes my knees. The sheets covering it are bunched in the middle as if slept in. More salt wafts from them, and something else… Male. Musk. Has he slept here?

"I warned you once never to ignore me," he hisses against the nape of my neck before shoving me once again.

I manage to throw my hands out at the last second, catching my fall. The position gives me enough leverage to twist onto my side so that I can face him. It's a habit I learned from Robert. Watching him is always my only defense. Only then could I guess his next move.

But this man is unreadable. When he snatches at my hip, I don't fight, letting him wrench the fabric of my robe loose. My only action is to flex my shoulders so that he can remove the garment without tearing it—out of courtesy to Vanya for sparing it. Within seconds, the black satin is in his fist before being tossed onto the floor.

Again, he eyes my body with unabashed interest—but I can't help but notice that his gaze doesn't assault the places where I'm used to being ogled. He eyes my stomach, not my breasts. My arms. Thighs. I know why. I can feel the marks throbbing after the rough treatment of the past twenty-four hours, but I don't dare focus on them.

I watch him instead. His wounds are much older than mine, scarred over and silvery with age. Battle scars. Gunshot wounds. He reminds me of the target in the fields where Robert likes to practice shooting. Dinged and marred but still unbroken.

"What's your name?" he asks, flicking the words at me one by one. Language to him is a projectile, used to inflict damage.

I cower. Everything I would have spilled easily to Vanya sticks in my throat.

Mischa lets nearly a minute go by before he entertains the fact that I might have disobeyed him. It amuses him rather than angers. His lips quirk around the edges, his eyelids lowering. With one knee, he nudges my right leg, making the space between both of them wider. A lazy shift of his weight allows him to dominate that vacant space. But he's too big. My inner thighs chafe against the coarse fabric of his pants. The air catches in my chest.

Vanya's warning becomes a mocking taunt: *He won't fuck you, but he'll still hit you.* He sounded sincere, but I know men. I learned long ago how to recognize the subtle ways their bodies tense. How their breathing changes when logic ends and lust begins.

But it's not my body that excites him.

It's the silence. The longer it extends between us, the bigger he seems, towering above. Defiance in general is unacceptable to most men like him. But from a woman?

He laughs, almost to himself: an unstable, guttural sound. "Did you not hear me, Little One?" Again, his fingers come to dance the length of my hip, but this time, they don't inspect the injuries there. They fan out, pressing firmly. *Feeling.* "He's treated you roughly. I can tell."

His hand is big enough to circle my entire thigh. Sensing the danger enclosed in his palm, I flinch, and in retaliation, the tips of his nails rake a path to my knee.

"But trust me: I can be worse. Tell me your name."

My lips flutter, but nothing comes out. Inhaling, I try again. Again. My tongue frantically moistens my lips as my chest heaves, seeking air. *My name is...*

Before I can form the words, his knee strikes the mattress near my hip, rattling the bed frame. The way he's positioned brings his thigh overtop mine, crushing me down. Heat sears, mingling with the sweat slicking my skin. It's too hot. Can't breathe...

"Tell me your name, Little One." He hasn't fully mounted me yet, remaining crouched instead. "Tell me what you know of Robert's plans and this will end for you. I swear it." He means it —as much as a man like him can mean anything. This is his idea of mercy: a painless death. "But if you don't..."

A gasp rips from my chest as he adjusts his knee, lifting it from the bed only to reposition it directly between my legs. He slams it forward, nudging my mound.

"I will make you wish I'd *only* killed you."

My vision swims as my lips struggle to part. My name is right *there*, wavering on the tip of my tongue. I try as hard as I can to spit it out. Ellen… Ellen…

But the only sound to reach my ears is the ominous creaking of the bed frame. The hand on my thigh becomes a razor, nails sinking deep. Scouring. Using that grip for leverage, he brings his weight forward, mounting me fully, lowering his chest against mine. My nipples scrape the cotton of his shirt while his breath assaults my cheek, scorching a trail down to my throat. He's too close. Too heavy. Too…raw.

There's no disguising the muscle straining beneath his clothing. Poor Vanya doesn't know his master as well as he thinks.

He's hard. Not hard enough to be of much use—at least not yet —but hard enough to feel against my thigh, too real for comfort. My thoughts scatter. Instinct kicks in. With Robert, there is only one way to survive his assaults: lie there motionless. Never react. Let him finish quickly. Lick my wounds in peace.

My body is already complying with the first step of that routine. I go limp, conforming beneath the stranger's body. My eyes focus somewhere beyond his head. I don't think. I don't feel. I just endure…

"Look at me."

An unexpected sensation disrupts my mental clarity. *Fire.* Unfamiliar heat trickles between my legs: his hand. Each knuckle traces the outlines of my mound. Once. Twice. I tense, anticipating brutality: for him to jam them in at once. Stretch me open. Prove his point.

Anything but another slow, teasing swipe that tugs on my spine like a string. Too harsh. Too sharp. Too soft.

"Look at me, Little One." He snarls the command into my ear, bringing his mouth so close that his teeth clip my earlobe.

The pain won't let me escape. It buzzes through my nerves like a fly until I have no choice. My vision refocuses, bringing his features into stark relief.

"You think I don't know?" he wonders coldly. "You think I can't see the abuse on you? You don't fear pain." He pinches my hip as if to prove it, rousing a deep, sharp ache that makes me shiver. "But there are some things worse than pain, Little One. Betrayals that only your body can commit against you. I won't just hurt you. I can make you *enjoy* what I do to you."

It's an almost cartoonish threat, but he never laughs. There's a sudden darkness to his features that wasn't there before. A harsh, knowing look that makes a part of me clench in despair. God, it's familiar. Understanding? The same expression worn by the boy who taught me how to endure agony in silence all those years ago.

He *knows*. What I've been through—or at least what he could discern from my scars. Even worse, he seems to think he can use that trauma against me. It's as laughable a boast as it is terrifying.

Breathe, Ellen. I make myself limp again, building an invisible wall between my body and my thoughts. I succeed. I feel nothing. Hear nothing. Just silence and…

Wet. Sliding along my breast, slicking the nipple. His thumb. While I watch, he brings the digit to his tongue and licks along the edge, wetting it further. Then he lowers it to my nipple again, letting his saliva merge with sweat. Disgust traps the air in my lungs, suffocating me during the long, deliberate journey he travels down the curve of my rib cage.

"W-what are you doing?" *No!* My own mental plea can't keep the words from leaving my throat. It's already too late.

He heard me, letting his fingers still against my torso. "So you *can* speak," he murmurs. "What a shame. I was beginning to suspect that your master had the perfect woman. Beautiful *and* quiet as a fucking mouse."

Vodka still taints his breath, but he isn't drunk. The look in his eyes is too hardened. Too steady. For the first time, I see the hint of real lust lurking in his heavy-lidded gaze. Chuckling, he slides his palm down to my hip and then underneath, cupping my buttock. My skin crawls. I can't look at him. The ceiling. *Feel nothing. Breathe, Ellen—*

"No." His free hand latches onto my scalp, forcing my face toward his and those soulless eyes. "You want to end this? Give me what I want. Or I'll just take it. "

He continues to touch me—and there is no blocking him out. Rough. Hard. Nails. Fingertips. My mind reels at how he interchanges brutality with...softness? Almost like a child flickering a light switch to disorient those trapped inside a locked room.

"I underestimated you," he proclaims, frowning as if disappointed by the fact. "Your master trained you too well."

Master. Trained. I can't explain the reaction those words set off in me. Heart stopping. Chilling. Mainly, they just trigger memories. Robert. Those awful nights. The hateful things he made me feel. Enduring him. Suffering him.

He never trained me to withstand him. All I had to cling to was one pathetic word. *Breathe.*

"Don't ignore me." My captor touches me again, grazing me more firmly with ragged nails. "I've been patient enough—"

"Stop." A stranger utters that plea—not me. I rarely say that word anymore. Only when Robert's at his worst. His cruelest. When I can barely think through the pain. But all I feel now is…

More heat prickling down my spine, fading between my legs. It's more alarming than pain. Too foreign to place. My hips roll of their own accord, desperate to escape it.

Unconcerned, the stranger continues to touch me, sliding his fingers from the curve of my hip, down between my legs. Each pass is bolder. Faster.

"S-stop!" My hand forms a fist without permission from my brain. Rises from the mattress. Strikes his shoulder. "Please—"

"Your name." The callous tone doesn't match the lazy sweep of his fingers against my flesh. Once. Twice. Again.

On the next pass, he curls his fingertips, teasing my entrance. Only the ragged tip of a nail breaches the barrier of my curls— but I feel the invasion deeper than just in my skin. In my heart, jagged and unwelcome like a rusty nail being jammed into a fortress I thought impenetrable for so long.

"S-stop." It's more than a broken whisper now. "Stop. Please."

His expression is unreadable, composed of fathomless eyes that watch me tremble without a shred of pity. Of mercy. "You want to end this, Little One?" he wonders, drawing his hand away. "Give me your name and all you know of Robert Winthorp."

My name. I try to remember through the chaos flooding my brain. The stranger has to compete with phantoms from memories. *Like sisters…like sisters…*

I can't find the answer in time. My punishment comes swiftly.

He presses more firmly with his finger, grazing flesh and nerves that shudder at the brazen display. Humiliation descends. My eyes burn. Tears gather, along with the knowledge that nothing I do can keep them from falling.

I can't even scream.

CHAPTER 6

"Give me your name, Little One. Say it, or I will make you scream—"

"Misha! We need to move. Now." That voice…

Hope, the fragile thing, rises in my chest as I make out the figure who appears in the doorway, his face half in shadow. Vanya.

"Mischa," he prods in a cautious tone directed at the man on top of me. "We need to go. Now."

"Is that so?" Eyes narrowed, Mischa shoves me aside and backs off the bed. Something terrible unfolds across his face, but I sense that it isn't all directed at Vanya—or even me. He stares down at his hands, flexing the fingers. Then he shakes his head and his expression is cold again. "And what could have happened so suddenly that we need to move base now?"

Vanya doesn't shy away from meeting his gaze. If anything, his chin juts slightly into the air, almost as if echoing their previous standoff but in reverse. *Are you challenging me?*

57

"You told me you trust my judgment. My judgment is telling me not to trust that snake Xavier with our location for too long. Besides, it's dark. The men are ready. This shithouse could crumble beneath us at any moment. I say we move now, to another safe house. Before it's too late."

"And her?" Mischa cocks his head toward me, his mouth tilted in a dangerous smirk that's more snarl than grin.

Vanya shrugs. "We bring her with us. You can continue your questioning later. It doesn't make sense to kill her now—"

"Oh?" Mischa reaches into his pocket and withdraws what I *actually* felt against my hip during his torture: a knife, thick at the base with a tapered tip. Light plays off the honed edges of the metal, stinging my eyes to the point where I have to blink. At that moment, he turns toward me, raising the blade. He's nearly to the bed when Vanya takes just a step in his wake.

"We don't have the time to hide her body—"

"Really?" Mischa wonders, chuckling when he doesn't receive an answer. "Relax. I will let you keep your toy, Vanya," he taunts, growling another hollow laugh. "You only need ask."

"I…" Vanya shakes his head dismissively. "You can deal with her later. We need to move now."

"Fine." Mischa heads for the door, sheathing his blade. As he passes Vanya, he deliberately nudges the man's shoulder with his, knocking him off balance. "Do what you wish, Ivan. But she is *not* Anna-Natalia—"

That name. It tugs on another memory. A name so beautiful that I strived to remember it, even though I only heard it uttered once, by a woman with a gentle, quivering voice years ago.

"I *will* question her later," Mischa says, snapping my attention back to him. His eyes narrow. He noticed my reaction. "Until then, she's your responsibility," he adds, still speaking to Vanya. "Whatever she does, you do, Vanya." He slips through the doorway and marches down the hall, but his voice reaches back to us, assaulting my fragile skin one last time. "I suggest you keep her in the cage."

"Here." Vanya approaches the bed and stoops to pick something up off the floor nearby. My robe. He hands it to me and averts his gaze while I hurry into it. "Stay close to me," he warns as my cheeks flush. "We need to go—"

"Wait." I reach for his arm without understanding why. He doesn't shove me off, which gives me enough time to regain control of my throat. "Ellen... My name is Ellen."

Confusion flickers across his face. Then he just nods. "Right. Let's go."

I stand and follow him into the hallway. The floor feels strangely slick beneath one foot. On top of that, I'm limping, subconsciously avoiding any pressure on my right heel. A quick glance down reveals blood coating the side of it. I must have stepped on the glass in the kitchen.

"We'll get that fixed later," Vanya says, noticing the blood as well. "Come."

We return to the main room, where roughly five men are in the process of taking what little items remain and carrying them down the hall. It's organized chaos with an air of routine underneath. These men are used to being on the move.

Vanya takes my wrist, pulling me along after him before I can wonder why. "Come." He reaches the kitchen through a different hallway. There, a man exits through a rickety screen door and we follow him, leaving the house altogether.

It's dark out. A blanket of stars coats an ebony night sky while a cold wind nips at the naked skin beneath my robe. Before us, an empty yard stretches for what seems like miles, closed in on either side by a wall of trees. It's quiet here. Too quiet. Craning my neck, I realize there are no other houses nearby. Just wilderness and silence.

"Have you lost your mind?"

A firm body brushes mine from behind. Before I can turn, my eyes are covered by something warm. Flesh. A hand?

"Go," my captor snarls—presumably at Vanya. I recognize his voice. *Mischa.* "I will keep her before you let her escape with enough intel to draw a fucking map for Winthorp."

He drags me in a different direction, heedless of how I stumble as my sore heel is aggravated. I'm forced against him, a slave to the motions of his body, my vision obscured. We don't go far, just paces from the house, over rugged terrain that crunches underfoot. Other footsteps catch my attention close by. Someone mutters something, but I can't make the words out. The language isn't English.

Suddenly, heat tickles my ear and the stench of vodka floods my nostrils.

"Get in," Mischa snarls.

I have only enough sense to throw my hand out in front of me before he shoves me forward. My fingers catch the edge of something firm. Metal. It's curved with space underneath for me to duck. My knees hit a ledge, which forces me to climb onto it. The seat of a vehicle, I think. The suspicion is proven correct when Mischa climbs in beside me, his bulk backing me against what must be the opposite door. Only now does he let me go, taking his hand off my face.

I'm not foolish enough to look up. Instead, I use stealth to discern our surroundings. Supple leather gives way beneath me —I was right. We're in the back seat of a van. The windows are tinted, letting in little light, and only one man occupies the front seat: the driver. I can't see his face, but he's wearing the same faded fatigues the other men are.

"Drive," Mischa tells him, tapping his fist against the window on his end. "Take up the rear. I'll keep watch."

He leans back against the seat, propping his arm along the headrest so that his reach extends beyond my neck. The tightness to his jaw betrays the otherwise casual motion. He's done it for my benefit, to remind me just how quickly he could regain control should I run.

Aware of him watching, I place my hands on my lap and face ahead. My heel stings. There's no doubt that I've tracked blood all over the floor of the vehicle. I do my best to keep the wound from contacting anything else, but the best way requires that I cross my legs with the injured heel dangling in the air. The motion puts my foot in his domain, close enough to his knee that I'll brush it with one good bump in the road.

Which is worse?

"Do not think that Vanya's pity can save you," Mischa says as if to warn me from even an accidental touch. "I have humored him this long. Besides, it's not you in particular that he cares for. He does it out of grief."

I can't help but wonder if he said that more to himself than to me. When my gaze flickers in his direction, I find him frowning and my heart beats faster in foreboding. A man like him secretes anger like sweat. It slicks his skin and floods the car, drowning me beneath the scent.

Suffocating me.

"You haven't asked why," he remarks after seconds pass in silence. Something battles with the malice in his tone, catching me off guard. Approval? "Perhaps your master trained you, after all."

I shudder at the mention of Robert. My master? He has a different word for it. I am only allowed to call him one thing, apart from his name. My thoughts shy from recalling it and I turn to the window, desperate to piece together the scenery.

Breathe, Ellen…

A hand seizes my jaw before I can make out anything more than shadow, wrenching me around to face the man beside me.

"You remind him of his daughter," he tells me. His gaze traps mine, probing deeply without mercy. He sees the way I flinch and interest flickers across his otherwise callous expression. "She was murdered years ago. Butchered. I think you know by who—"

"Sir?" the driver calls as he wrenches on the wheel. Too fast.

The sudden shift throws me in Mischa's direction. In disgust, he shoves me off, twisting around to gaze from the back windshield. Whatever he sees makes his face fall flat.

"Shit. Get down!"

There's an eerie moment when all I hear is the roar of an engine. My gaze meets a pair of amber irises staring back, and for the first time, something other than hate is reflected in them.

Fear.

"Get down!"

Wham! Everything happens too quickly to decipher. Clanging noise. Shattering glass. Darkness. Pain.

A thunderous roar rattles through my being, and then...*slam!* Air wheezes from my chest—I'm being crushed. Whatever it is pins me into the sliver of space between the front and back seats. Metal?

No...a *body*.

A guttural voice snarls something into my ear, but only snippets register. "Down—stay down!"

Sharp noises cut the air. *Gunshots.* They echo in tandem. At least twenty right after the other.

Bang!

Bang!

Bang!

Then nothing.

"Vlad?" Misha shouts through the resounding quiet.

A groan comes from the front seat. "I...I'm alright."

"Good. Then drive!" Crouched beside me, Mischa rummages through his pocket, withdrawing something that he aims in the air. "I'll cover you."

Predatory. That's the only way to describe how he maneuvers swiftly into the seat, aiming at something unseen through the window. The *shattered* window.

Glass speckles the seat, glimmering in my hair and over the satin of my robe. Did we hit something? In the darkness, I make out the edge of what seems to be a dirt road. The windshield is cracked, but branches extend beyond it, casting shadows over the hood. A tree—we must have run into it.

When the driver tries to reverse, the engine squeals and then dies.

"Shit." Keeping low, Mischa nudges the door beside me open. Before I can even think to escape, his fingers clench my shoulder. "Move without my say so and I'll kill you." A cold, round object taps the side of my skull as a deadly reinforcement. "Go."

With him on my heels, I climb from the wreckage.

It quickly becomes apparent that we aren't alone. Three other vans are stalled up ahead. Each one sits askew, as if their drivers had to slam on the brakes to stop suddenly. Men exit them. When they see Mischa, one of them shouts words I can't discern.

Then…gunshots.

"Get down!"

I'm shoved to the earth and crushed once again. This time, I can hear the breathing of the man on top of me. It's steady despite the tumult of noise happening around us. More people shout. More gunshots ring out.

"Get up!"

The pressure lifts from off me, and I barely manage to suck in a breath before I'm being dragged into the shadows that line the roads. Grass prickles my feet. Shadows flicker in the darkness. Near. Far.

Another gunshot rings out, way too close for comfort.

And then a man appears from behind a tree up ahead. He's armed, pointing a gun squarely in my direction. His clothes stick out to me as fear grips my lungs—he's not wearing fatigues. Instead, a crisp suit clashes with the wilderness around us. His gun isn't large and bulky either but sleek. A pistol. His face…

I know it—the hazy kind of recognition that comes only from a glance.

And he knows me.

His eyes widen. Quickly, his free hand goes to his ear. "She's alive. I found her! She—"

Thunder roars nearby, deafening me as blood flies from the man's head. He falls and my brain belatedly names the reason why. *He's dead.*

"Move."

The grip on my arm turns brutal, crunching bone and twisting flesh. Changing direction, Mischa steers me to the road, keeping his gun at the ready. From the acrid smell tickling my nostrils, I know he is the one who shot the other man. If any more enemies are lurking nearby, they must have been dispatched. Only his men remain, their weapons drawn…

Or their bodies lying prone and lifeless.

"Fuck." Mischa spits on the ground, his face drawn tight. When we come close enough, he shoves me toward someone, and the man catches me, gripping my shoulders. "Go. Get her to the safe house."

The way he said it… My body trembles at the unspoken warning. He saw it too. He heard it. Those were not generic mercenaries.

"Go!"

My new captor steers me toward an open van and hastens in after me. Vanya. His face is drawn tight, and I stiffen when he reaches over me.

"Your seat belt," he prompts, shoving the bit of metal into my hand and nodding toward the base. "Put it on."

I obey and the van lurches into motion, presumably heading toward even more danger.

CHAPTER 7

Whether by accident or intent, Vanya doesn't cover my eyes, and I'm allowed to witness the entire trip through winding fields and hills. It's desolate here, somewhere in the countryside, far from the airport. The thought makes my stomach clench in a way that has nothing to do with fear. Just pain. Just guilt.

As Mischa claimed, I was just a decoy. Though, assuming she was aware of the switch, would Briar fare any better in my situation? Sweet, playful Briar who couldn't even go five minutes without a friend to chat with or sycophants to entertain. I've seen her charm Robert Sr. in his foulest of moods, always getting her way. Could she enthrall this murderer with hell in his eyes and a million scars written upon his skin?

I have no shame in admitting that, yes, she probably could. Men always fell for Briar. Fought for her. Fought *over* her.

But there is one man who will fight for you, a part of me hisses. *Whether you want him to or not.*

Robert.

I cringe from the thought and turn to the window, desperate for a distraction. I find one. Hell stares back at me. Dark eyes meet mine coldly through the glass as the door is unceremoniously opened. He doesn't reach for my hand, but my *hair*, wrenching me out by my scalp. Through watering eyes, I can only assume we've arrived at the "safe house" by the gravel at my feet and the shadow of a building ahead.

The air here reeks of copper. There's little light to see by, and inside the structure, cold floors betray a sense of abandonment. I'm not sure how far we've traveled before he releases me so suddenly that I fall to my knees. A ratty, threadbare carpet beneath me coughs up dust with every movement made upon it. Only one other person occupies this room, pacing the length of the floor.

"Who are you?" His voice is low, but it somehow still manages to echo to the far reaches of the room.

A single light fixture illuminates the narrow space: another decaying cage of wood coated with brown wallpaper this time. The windows here aren't boarded up. Blurred glass displays my reflection: wide-eyed and trembling.

Who am I? I'm not sure the woman staring back at me even knows.

"Those were *Winthorp's* men," the man in front of me continues. "You are not Briar." He tosses me a calculating glance as if to make sure of that fact. "So who are you? Robert only has two children."

I can see him trying to put the pieces together on his own. When he looks at me again, his eyebrow is raised, but he shakes his head as if to cut off his own thought. Not a Winthorp by blood. So who?

"What is your name?"

"Ellen." The voice isn't mine, and I turn to find Vanya standing in the doorway. There's blood on his chin. His? Or someone else's, smeared there during the attack? "Her name is Ellen," he says again, the words rushed. "She—"

"Leave us," Mischa says sharply. He jerks his chin in dismissal but Vanya remains.

"Mischa." There's a plea tucked into the name this time. Something emphatic, more than just concern for me. *Don't do this.* "She's just a woman—"

"A woman who nearly got us all killed." Mischa reaches into his pocket and withdraws his knife, letting the blade catch the light. "I told you to leave us once, Ivan. Do not make me tell you twice."

Seconds crawl by until reluctant footsteps finally retreat down the hall. My heart aches in Vanya's absence, hammering against the wall of my rib cage. But I can't take my gaze off the knife.

As if aware of that fact, Mischa crouches on one knee and brings the blade near my jawline. Sharpened metal tickles my cheek, stinging. Slicing. All the while, his eyes stare into mine, hunting down the confessions I haven't voiced.

"Who. Are. You? Not an innocent after all? One of their spies?"

An answer is on the tip of my tongue. *No one.* My lips twitch to voice it. Too late.

Those amber irises darken with violent intent, but I only see his arm twitch before...*pain!* I instinctively clutch the side of my face with one hand as my brain struggles to process the sensations battling for attention. Burning. Searing. Wide-eyed, I watch scarlet drops dribble onto my chest. My thighs. The floor.

"I just lost three men because of you," Mischa warns, sounding miles away. His tone has changed in a heartbeat. There's no anger. Just grim acceptance that conveys the inevitable. He'll do it now. Kill me. "Answer me."

The knife grazes my throat next, biting deeper when I flinch.

"P-please." I don't recognize the plaintive voice that comes out of me. I don't know why I resist him at all. Dying would be easier than suffering him. Dying would be preferable to returning to Robert.

Though maybe not. Barely a day from Winthorp manor and something I thought I'd never feel again floods my veins. It's weak, hardly strong enough to outlast the fear, but still there. *Survival.*

"My name is Ellen—"

"I don't give a damn about your name," Mischa growls, and the knife cuts deeper. More burning. Stinging.

A whimper escapes my throat, but nothing registers over his features. No pity. No humanity. Nothing.

"Who are you?"

"My name is Ellen Winthorp," I stammer through the pain. "Ellen *Winthorp.*"

The blade stills. Withdraws. "How?"

Shaking, I force myself to meet his gaze directly. More tears sting my eyes and I let them fall, forsaking any attempts to hide the truth. "I…I am Robert's wife."

CHAPTER 8

Robert's wife. I don't think I've ever said those words out loud. At least not to another person. In my old world, they would have been met with something akin to pity and decorum. A tight nod perhaps. Or maybe a sympathetic pat on my hand. Not disgust. Not revulsion so potent that I taste it on my tongue.

"His wife?" He mulls the title over, deciding within an instant that it must be a lie. His pupils constrict menacingly. "Robert Sr. has no wife—"

"Not him." I shake my head, too tired to specify.

"His son?"

I just nod.

"You're lying."

My body stiffens at his tone, but I'm not quick enough to cower beyond his reach. He grabs me, his fingers clenching the back of my scalp, twisting through my hair.

73

"*He* doesn't have a wife, either. And I doubt that he would let her be used as a decoy."

It's a question I haven't let myself think on. Has Robert grown tired of me? Or has his father finally sought to put an end to his son's obsession?

Both scenarios are equally alarming.

"You wear no ring," Mischa adds, jerking his chin toward my naked hand. "I know of every goddamn Winthorp for generations, and I've never heard your name before."

"I-I'm not…approved." It's the only thing I can think to say. The only explanation that doesn't require divulging the full truth. Perhaps I'm not that desperate to live after all? Some wounds aren't worth reopening. Some horrors can't be faced alone.

Regardless, the answer seems to satisfy my captor. He frowns, and I can tell from the grudging set to his jaw that he'll believe that much at least: that the defiant son of Robert Winthorp Sr. would take a wife without his notorious father's permission. After all, there is one undisputable fact this night has proven.

"He sent his men after you," Mischa says, obviously annoyed by what he can't explain. Something bright and terrible flits across his gaze, illuminating the irises. Before I can blink, the knife returns. "He's willing to kill for you. And you shall return to him in *pieces*."

Pain! Fire sears through my skull: the result of another cut slicing right through the first. Instinct takes hold of my body. I try to turn away, but his free hand grips my scalp tighter, holding me in place while he raises the blade again. He lets me see the tip of it, painted red with my blood. Then he lashes out, piercing the meat of my cheek, down my jaw.

"You are number fifteen," he tells me over my whimper.

Somehow, I'm still fully aware as he makes another cut, angled toward the first. God, it hurts—just like he wants it to. He takes his time, slicing through flesh bit by bit. And I see lightning. My eyes flood and overflow. I'm shaking in his grip as air escapes my lungs in a pathetic, wheezing gasp.

"The fifteenth martyr in a blood war," he continues, his voice wavering.

At first, I assume it's because I'm delirious. Dizzy. But no… I see his throat jerk as he swallows hard. There's an unsteadiness to his grip that I didn't notice before—I'm not shaking on my own.

"You may be an innocent in this, but I will kill you, Ellen Winthorp," he promises me, negating any suspicion that what he feels might be guilt. No. He's resigned to my murder. "But not yet."

He pushes me to the floor and leaves me here, bleeding over the carpet. I count his footsteps as they fade somewhere deeper inside the house. When that sound trails off…I count my heartbeat.

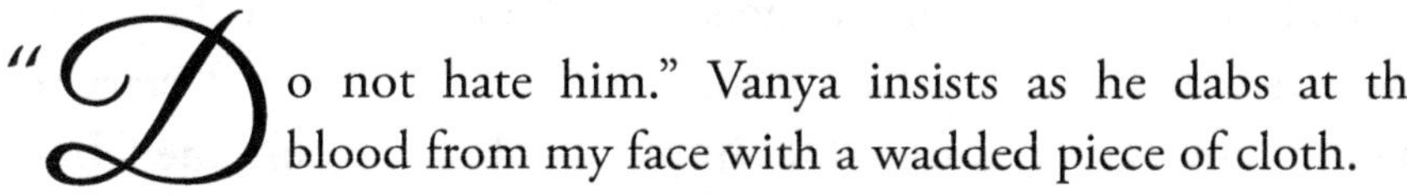

"*D*o not hate him." Vanya insists as he dabs at the blood from my face with a wadded piece of cloth.

Is he speaking to me or himself? I can't tell. I'm not sure when the older man returned to find me, bleeding and broken, either. All I know is partial relief as he treats my wounds.

"It's not you he hates. He wasn't always this way," he admits almost reluctantly. "There was a time when he'd never... Do not hate him."

Is hate what I feel for the newest monster to mutilate my body? I'm not sure. Maybe I just don't care enough to define it. Every man has a story to explain away the demons that eventually consume him. I've learned the history of one. I'm not keen to learn another.

But more than his violence troubles Vanya about his leader. Frowning, he draws the cloth away and reaches for a pack of gauze. Inside is a square piece of bandage, which he places over my left cheek and secures with tape. Then he sighs. "You are my responsibility," he says, changing the subject. "I do not want to bind you. Or lock you in the cage."

I can't swallow my sigh of relief. "Thank—"

"*But*," he says over me, "I will if I have to. What you do reflects on me. Do you understand?"

I nod.

"Good." He stands, wincing once he's on his feet. From this angle, it's not hard to see why. Blood cakes the side of his face near his ear.

Something soft strikes my fingers and I look down and find that I've reached for the cloth without realizing it. When I start to stand, Vanya says nothing. He simply watches as I raise the fabric in a trembling fist and dab it along his ear. He's too tall. I have to stand on tiptoe to clean the wound properly. Underneath all the blood is only a hairline scratch, caused by glass I presume.

Rather than thank me, Vanya snatches the cloth and tosses it aside. Then he gathers up the rest of his supplies and heads for the doorway. "You'll stay in here. I'll try to find you a blanket, but I suggest you make do until then. I'll keep watch outside the door. Get some sleep."

Gratitude renders me speechless. By the time I remember how to speak, he's already gone, closing the door to the room after him. Unless my ears play tricks, I hear the lock engage. Oddly enough, I feel safer here than at any other point in this nightmare. I don't care to decipher the reasons for his kindness. Maybe they're entirely selfish, as Mischa insinuated.

Still…

No matter how small, the mercy is rare enough to be cherished.

At least without wondering how long it may last.

*V*ibrations draw me awake. Footsteps? Gasping, I open my eyes to an unfamiliar ceiling and a chillingly familiar silhouette.

"I changed my mind," Mischa declares. "Get up."

He heads for the door, leaving me to follow. Limping, I struggle to keep up before he can issue a threat not to fall behind. Pale daylight spills in through the window, illuminating part of the narrow hall while leaving the rest of the house bathed in shadow.

It's older than the last one, with rotting floorboards and a smaller floor plan. The men seem to be spread throughout rather than grouped in one room. They keep their guns close and linger near windows. Searching.

Up a rickety staircase are two rooms. I spy a bed in one, but I'm herded toward another. Small and confined, the space contains a card table surrounded by mismatched chairs. Black sheets shroud the windows, and a single lamp in the corner casts dingy yellow light.

"Sit." Mischa nods his chin toward the metal folding chair closest to me.

Aware of him watching my every move, I lower myself slowly, keeping my gaze trained on my imminent surroundings. There is nothing else in this room. In fact, it appears to have no purpose other than this: silence, isolation.

"Look at me, Ellen Winthorp."

He's seated across from me. Shadows distort his features, making his eyes seem darker, his face narrower. Hollow.

Without warning, he reaches toward me, sliding a finger along the gauze taped to my cheek. "Have you seen your face?"

There's a taunt tucked into the question. Beneath the bandage, the wound sears, reacting to his nearness. One of his knuckles deliberately nudges the area that feels the deepest and I hiss in response.

"Take the bandage off."

My fingers shake as I obey, carefully undoing Vanya's handiwork.

"Look." He places something on the table and shoves it toward me. A mirror, small and round, with a crack in the glass.

I lift it, seeking enough light to make out my reflection. A haunted ghost stares back, her blue eyes wide and empty. Blood coats the left side of her face, running in rivulets down her throat. I swallow hard at the sight, but that's not what he wanted me to see.

It's the shape of the wound. Careful. Intentional. I have to tilt my jaw to make it out fully. From beneath my eye all the way down to my jaw, he carved an X. Beside it, extending toward my ear, is a jaggedly sliced letter V. The nonsensical doodles of a madman?

I almost assume as much until I recall what he said. *You are number fifteen.* XV. He marked my fate in Roman numerals. If I live long enough for the wounds to heal, they will leave scars proclaiming my fate forever.

"Look at me."

I lower the mirror and find him watching me. There's no hiding beneath his gaze. Heat wells behind my eyes and spills out. Each tear sinks into the rent skin, setting the flesh on fire. I don't turn away from him or try to disguise the pain, however. I let him see it.

And he should relish this moment. His jaw clenches as he tracks the descent of every drop of moisture. Every wince. Does it justify his hatred? Feed his rage? For once, I can't tell.

"How did you meet your husband?"

I look down, recoiling from that word. *Husband.* The action irritates my captor.

He seizes my chin. "Look at me." He jerks my face toward his, tightening his grip so that I have no choice but to meet his gaze. Emptiness stares back.

I always thought Robert had no soul, but even he could feign humanity when he wanted to. *What do you think I'd do without you, Ellen?* he'd growl every now and then. *You keep me sane. Don't you fucking see?*

"Answer me, Little One." My new tormentor has had to repeat himself. Irritation sparks from those fathomless irises, prickling my skin. "Your husband. How did you meet him? I know Robert has a fondness for whores."

I stifle my reaction to the insinuation. Whore. If only. At least, then, I would have earned something from my endeavor. I could have justified it.

"I grew up in Winthorp manor," I say. Speaking hurts. Even the slightest movement of my jaw triggers more wet warmth to drip onto my collar.

"As a maid?" Mischa questions.

Still restrained by his grip on my chin, I nod.

"Really?" He lets me go and rises to his feet, circling toward my side with effortless speed. He has the knife again and lowers the blade so that I can see it, cleaned from the night before and ready to inflict more damage. "Lie to me again, Ellen, and your pretty face will be nothing more than a painful memory. Understand?"

"Y-yes—"

"Then tell me who you are. Really."

"I-I wasn't lying," I insist. "I *did* grow up in the manor."

"But as a *maid?*"

"N-not officially—"

"Don't mince words with me." His fingers flex against the knife's handle in a warning. "If not a maid, then as what?"

I run through those memories, trying to put my role into words that don't sting. Something that doesn't require further questioning.

"My mother was…close to the Winthorps. When she died, they kept me around as Briar's companion." I hold my breath as he digests that explanation.

Relief renders me boneless when his hand finally withdraws.

"And?" he presses.

"When I grew older, Robert…noticed me." My throat tightens and I leave it at that. Not even the threat from the blade can draw out more.

Thankfully, Mischa doesn't seem to give a damn either way. Robert. That name acts as a trigger to whatever evil lurks within him. His face becomes that fearsome mask once again, reducing him to more monster than human.

"And you married him?" He stands back, watching me with an expression I can't decipher. Disgust?

Or something more terrifying: *suspicion.*

"Stepanov," he says quietly. "Do you know that name?"

I shake my head.

"Really?" The man lifts an eyebrow, unconvinced. "You've never heard your husband say it?"

"He doesn't talk about business around me."

"Oh?" Two heavy footsteps bring him closer. Slowly, he sinks to his knees, down to my level. "What about the *Mafiya*? The *Pakhan*? Do those ring a bell?"

The corner of his mouth quirks when I shake my head, but it's not a smile.

"What about…" He leans in close, allowing his breath to nuzzle my bleeding wounds. When I shiver, he trails his thumb along my cheek and withdraws it, painted red. "What about Anna-Natalia Vasilev? Does *that* name ring a bell?"

I jump instinctively. There's no hiding it. I'm sure the memory that name triggers unfolds across my face just as strongly as it does in my mind.

It was so long ago that I shouldn't be able to recall her so clearly. She was thin. Small. Her hair was long and dark, like Vanya's might have been once. Her upturned eyes were a delicate shade of brown.

And she was in chains.

"I only saw her once."

There's no point in lying to him. He knows. There's something predatory in him that hunts through my pain, drawing the truth out whether I like it or not. Maybe it's what I think I find lurking beneath all the hate and rage. Desperation?

Do not hate him, Vanya insisted. *He wasn't always this way.*

"Where?" His tone makes me suspect he already knows the answer.

"Winthorp Manor," I croak through my pain. "Robert Sr. had her…in a basement. I was young. Maybe seven? His son had me bring her water—"

"Why?" He slams his fist against the table out of anger more than emphasis. *Again,* he already knows the answer.

Tasting blood, I tell him. "I don't know—"

"Did you see her die?"

I blink, thrown off by the question. Do you need to see the killing blow to witness someone die? Not necessarily. Death can be a slow process, tracked only by a steady change in your reflection day after day. Or a look in the eye. I picture the woman, Anna-Natalia. Was she dead then, huddled in chains at the mercy of the Winthorps?

"N-no—"

"Do you want to hear how they did it?"

My heart hammers against my chest as I shake my head emphatically. *No.* They butchered her, he claims. I've seen firsthand what Robert does to animals for sport. He hunts them. Guts them. He shows them no mercy.

Mischa comes in close so that his words slither directly into my ear. "They slit her throat. Then they cut off her hands and sent them to her father in a box. She was sixteen."

I gag at the imagery. Those beautiful eyes open and unseeing. Her pain. Her fear.

"Her body, they dumped into the river. Unlike you, she was an innocent in this. She was number twelve."

Twelve. A martyr in a blood war, he said. But the only wars I knew of were the internal ones raging through the Winthorp estate. Father against son. Brother against sister. Gossip. Intrigue. Jealousy. Anna-Natalia Vasilev never cracked the dinner table chatter.

In fact… The only figure to ever intrude upon the sanctity of the manor was a boy who snuck into my room in the dead of night. His eyes burned through the darkness, his voice a hiss. Even then, so young, I knew he'd kill me. There was a knife in his hand and murder in his soul.

Though, for whatever reason, *that* monster let me go.

But I don't tell Mischa that. Something he said keeps echoing in my thoughts, intriguing me enough to voice it. "T-twelve?"

He frowns at my pathetic attempts at probing. Still, he tosses me a bone. "Your husband's family has a long list of sins, Little One," he tells me. "A very long list. We keep track of the victims related by blood." Almost gingerly, he fingers a piece of my hair, lifting it for inspection in the dim lighting. I don't expect the moment he tugs hard, drawing a whine from my lips. "But his transgressions are nothing compared to mine." He returns to his full height and kicks the leg of my chair. "Get up."

The world spins when I do. Pain and exhaustion play a violent game for supremacy over my battered body.

I stagger on my feet when he takes my hand and drags me into the hall. Rather than head for the stairs, he shoves me toward the room next door. Oh, God. It's the one with the bed and another window, nailed shut. A mocking view of an empty field greets me beyond it. Outside, the sky is a dreary, stormy gray. How many days has it been so far? I can't tell.

"Don't get any cute ideas, Little One." Mischa cups my chin, forcing me to face him. "In fact...I *dare* you to run from me."

His eyes glow at the threat of a chase. Here and now, I make the decision never to take him up on that challenge.

"You *do* look like her. You're just as beautiful," he admits, almost to himself. His finger drifts up my jawline and comes away red. Meeting my gaze, he swipes his tongue along the pad of it. "But are you worth as much?"

His hands capture the ends of my robe. Aware of my terror, he takes his time, peeling the panels back, relishing how I shudder with every inch of skin revealed. When he finally undoes the sash, I don't resist. I lift my arms, letting him strip me down to nothing.

Then I watch him toss the satin onto the floor.

His gaze sweeps over my body, shamelessly logging every flaw and pore. Beautiful like Briar, he said? I'm not sure if he still has that opinion by the time our eyes reconnect.

"Lie down."

His voice seizes control of my limbs, and I take two steps back until my calves strike the mattress. Still facing him, I start to lower myself, but he frowns, irritated. Then he crosses the distance between us and shoves me down himself. Dazed, I blink up at the ceiling, tasting more blood on my tongue as wetness coats my neck. I'll ruin his sheets, but something tells me he doesn't mind.

He watches me bleed, nodding in satisfaction. "I want you to think about your husband, Little One," he says. "I want you to remember every twisted, sordid thing he's done to your body. Every way he's used you…"

It's a terrible request. My mind has more than enough ammunition to spawn a million nightmares. But does he know that? Looking at him, I can't tell. Maybe consent is such a foreign concept to him that he takes it for granted that most men ignore it altogether.

"Now…imagine me doing those things to you. All of them. Every last one." The malice in his voice doesn't match the involuntary way his eyes flicker across my naked chest. Quickly. As if nothing holds his interest—or he doesn't want it to. "Think about it until I come back and I hope you reconsider your silence."

Despair renders me boneless as he leaves the room, locking the door behind him. Then…something twisted enough to call amusement sets in. Imagine him as Robert? It's as easy as swapping out one monster for another. Or is it?

My eyes shut against the memories, but nothing short of unconsciousness can keep them at bay. My husband dishes out pain in exchange for his pleasure, and he *never* let me forget my role: *his*. When he touches me, I feel nothing but shame. Fear. Panic.

Never…fire. This man inspires a new terror I don't know how to fathom. I've grown so used to Robert. I can endure his routine. I can survive his games—Mischa is a dangerous anomaly. Were I given the choice between the two of them, is it really that hard to pick who I'd prefer?

No. I'd pick Robert. The known is always better than the unknown.

Always.

CHAPTER 9

The lumpy mattress beneath me reeks of mold, but I can't resist its comfort for long. When my eyes flutter open to a darkened room, I'm not sure how much time has passed. An hour? Longer? The darkness beyond the window doesn't reveal any answers. Neither do my sore, aching limbs, which throb as though I never slept at all.

My face, however, feels stiff. Sticky. The wounds have stopped bleeding from what I can tell, but each laceration burns with a new kind of pain. Robert always took care never to scar my face. He'd strike me, but always with an open hand.

What would he think to see me so ruined?

I trace the wounds with my finger, following the jagged contours that form my new title. Fifteen. *XV.* Does the reality of a new scar sadden me? I can't tell. Every instinct in my body warns that I won't live long enough to care.

As if the thought of mortality is their cue, footsteps approach the room. *His.* I sense him behind the door seconds later, lingering there as if aware of the unbearable anticipation building in my body.

He savors it. How it gets harder to breathe. How my nipples tighten in the still air, knowing that they'll be under his scrutiny soon. Humiliation is his greatest weapon, and he hones it for what feels like hours on my already frayed nerves.

"Get up."

I nearly sigh in relief when he finally kicks the door open and switches an overhead light on. Rather than smug, he looks…cold.

"This is my last offer of mercy: Will you tell me what you know of Robert Winthorp?"

I swallow down a lump of dread. "I know nothing."

"Fine." An expression distorts his mouth, which causes my heart to sink. Disappointment? "Then get dressed." He tosses something onto the floor near the bed.

Then I realize the position I'm in. How he finds me: twisted in the sheets on my side, my hair tangled around my shoulders. In sleep, my body forgot all about being a prisoner, seeking out the most comfortable position.

I have to take my time detangling my limbs before I can stand. My cheeks burn from more than just pain and I don't dare look up to see his reaction.

Instead, I stoop for the pile of fabric nearby. It's soft. Not a robe, but a thin negligee—though, where Vanya gave me clothing to preserve my modesty, this black creation of lace and silk is meant to entice. Or shame.

"Put it on."

I do without comment, surprised that the garment reaches past my knees. When Mischa observes me, I don't blush. Frowning, he turns away, shrugging his shoulder in a silent command for me to follow.

The cramped house is shrouded in darkness. I can hear other men moving throughout, but with Mischa in front of me, my vision is reduced to what little of the floor separates us. We pass through a doorway somewhere on the lower level and then descend a set of wooden stairs hammered into a concrete wall. A basement. My new cell?

There's little light here, but enough to make out another card table in the corner, where two men are sitting. One of them I recognize. Xavier, the man with the briefcase filled with money. He's wearing another suit and sitting tall, his hands folded neatly on his lap.

Sitting beside him, a balding stranger is wearing a black dress shirt and slacks. He eyes me boldly, drinking in the battered flesh beneath the hem of my shift. A pink tongue shoots out along his lips and he nods to no one in particular.

"I see what you mean, *Pakhan*," he says to Mischa. "They could be twins. But ah!" He tsks between his teeth and sadly shakes his head. "You've marred her already."

"Which shouldn't keep you from fucking her."

The words stop me dead in my tracks—not that my captor notices. He approaches the table while I shy back against the wall, pressing myself against the concrete.

"Name your price," Mischa demands, sending my heart into a frantic race against my thoughts. *Fucking her. Fucking her.*

The balding man smirks and casts another searing glance in my direction. Then he sighs, turning back to Xavier. "Business first. Tell your accountant here that my goods still sell for their going rate."

Mischa nods and Xavier lifts yet another briefcase from the floor and places it onto the table. This time, he sets something square, made of gray plastic, down as well. A scale of some kind? When he withdraws a stack of money, he removes the rubber band and sets the bills on the electronic device. He does that with five whole stacks and then looks to Mischa as if for approval.

"Take your goddamn blood money, Boris," Mischa snaps, but his voice lacks any real passion. When he cocks his head in my direction, my heart sputters. I make out only a sliver of his expression, the rest of his face is bathed in shadow. "Now, name your price."

For me.

Boris sits back and forms a steeple with his fingers as if thinking over the amount—but I can tell he already has a price in mind. "Just one night with Robert's bitch? Five thousand."

Mischa shrugs. "Done." There's something in how he says that word that sends alarm shooting down my spine. Distracted. Disinterested. There's no mocking ownership of his captive. No haggling. Like he's in a hurry to foist his cruelty onto someone else.

Someone who can do the job, a part of me whispers.

"Where can I have her?" Boris wonders as Xavier begins to reorganize his stacks of bills. Maybe focusing on him is the only way I can keep any sanity. His hands. How they shake…

"Upstairs," Mischa commands, his voice faint and distorted.

Blood rushes through my ears, counting the seconds that tick by. One heartbeat. Another. There's no time to think. Just survive.

Breathe, Ellen. Move, Ellen!

"W-wait!" I stagger forward, stupidly grasping Mischa's forearm.

His reaction is near instantaneous. *Wham!* I'm on my knees, enthralled by a million stars bouncing across my vision. They sparkle as my fingers clutch the right side of my face. It's numb. I taste blood. My ears ring.

"Take her upstairs," Mischa snarls. "Get her the fuck out of my sight—"

"No!" I move on instinct, following the sound of his voice with my fingers. They brush scalding muscle hidden beneath harsh material. His hip? "Wait!" The world swims around me as I stagger to my feet. Speaking is suddenly an ordeal. My jaw won't move the way it should, and every attempt sounds thick. Muted. "Wait. I can be of more use to you than—"

A hand clenches my throat, shoving me back against the wall. Mischa's. He pins me there without mercy, his face a terrifying snarl. There's no life in his eyes. Just darkness. Rage. Pain. "You're lucky I haven't killed you—"

"I can be more useful to you than as a whore," I rasp, fighting against my own tongue to sound intelligible. Human. He's reduced me to a creature that spits blood when she talks. My vision is blurred in my right eye. He's a smeared specter of light and shadow, but fear is a funny thing. It turns out to be no match against a deeper, more ingrained instinct: survival. "I can help you—"

"Shut up!" His fingers tighten, cutting off all air.

There's only enough left in my throat for two words. "He's…cheated…"

Confusion. It flits across his face so quickly that I almost miss it. But then his grip loosens and I don't wait for him to change his mind.

"He's cheated you," I croak, jerking my chin toward the table. "There's something wrong with the money—"

"Bitch." Mischa laughs, chuckling at the absurdity of it all. "You have permission to use force with her," he tells Boris from over his shoulder. "This whore has a smart little mouth."

"Just don't damage it too much," Boris replies. "You hit her again and I'll knock a grand off my price—"

"Listen to me!"

Shock registers across my captor's face, which is how I realize I screamed at him. Pleaded. *Listen*!

I've never said that to anyone. There was no use before. Ellen Winthorp was either a doll on display or a secret to be hidden. She had nothing to say and even fewer people who might care to hear it.

He has no choice but to listen to me now.

"I saw him," I blurt, forcing out the words as quickly as I can. "The bills. Ask him to weigh them—"

"Enough!" Mischa snarls. "I suggest you shut the fuck up—"

"Ask him to weigh the damn money!" I'm panting with the effort it takes to speak. My chest hurts. My face is a conflicting mixture of searing fire and throbbing ice. My eye must be swelling. It's impossible to keep it open, which gives me only a fraction of my normal field of vision to gauge his reaction from. By his side, his hand clenches into a fist and I stiffen in anticipation of the next blow. "Please—"

"Xavier," he snarls to the man at the table. "Do you have a different scale?"

The man fidgets, tugging on the collar of his suit. "Of course. Why?"

Mischa's eyes narrow into slivers. "Take it out."

When he turns, he drags me by my hair and shoves me against the table, rattling the bills stacked neatly there. "Show me."

Xavier recoils as my blood speckles the pristine rows of dollar bills. "What in God's name?"

Mischa doesn't answer him. He speaks only to me, twisting his fingers painfully through my hair. "Show me."

I reach for bills at random, searching for any clue as to their value. Something subtle… Or maybe I missed it? No, *there*. I lift a bill with a slight discoloration from the rest. Even through blurred, unfocused vision, I notice the abnormality. The green is a shade *too* bright, and the bill feels different from how it should. Brittle.

"Th-this one." I give the bill to Mischa, who hesitates only a second before snatching it.

"Weigh it," he tells Xavier, but the other man just laughs.

"*Pakhan*? Are you seriously humoring this—"

"Now." Mischa slams the bill onto the table so hard that the legs buckle, toppling over what precarious stacks of money remain. "Weigh. It."

Slowly, Xavier places it onto one side of an old-fashioned metal scale. He reaches for another bill, but I shake my head and fumble through the crumpled, blood-soaked paper myself.

Finally, my fingers find what I'm searching for. "This one."

Without a word, Mischa jerks his chin toward the scale, and I place the bill on the other end. Droplets of blood speckle both sides, but there is no mistaking the fact that one bill is obviously heavier than the other. The scale tilts a fraction of an inch.

And, suddenly, the air in the room loses all sense of stiff professionalism. Nothing riles men like money.

"Th-the bitch got them wet," Xavier says, his voice wavering only slightly. "Of course that will skew the—"

"Do it again." At his normal volume, Mischa sounds gruff. Dangerous. Now? Thunder resonates in every word, echoing down my spine. His fingers tighten around a chunk of my hair to convey a warning. *If you are wrong, I will kill you.* "Do it," he commands when Xavier hesitates. "But *she* chooses."

I blink my good eye and put all of my energy into focusing on the sea of green beneath my fingertips. Am I right? Have I just gambled my life away? The questions crowd my thoughts, nearly drowning out the senses that catch the irregularities in one bill. Another. Desperately, I point a shaking finger at them both and Xavier races to clear the scale before placing them on either side. Slowly. Reluctantly.

There's a heart-stopping second as the scale wavers. Up. Down. Balances…dips to one end. *Bingo*, as Robert would say. Both bills are fresh and clear of blood. There's no denying it this time.

As the revelation registers between the three men, the tension boils over. Spills.

"You thought you could steal from me?" Mischa shoves me aside and circles the table as Xavier backs himself into a corner.

"I-I don't know," Xavier stammers, desperate to find a narrative to save his life.

But it's too late. Mischa draws his knife…

And I turn away, stumbling in the dark until I hit the wall. Guilt. Fear. I feel all of it, inescapable even when I slam my hands over my ears and hum to drown out what happens next. La, la, la—it's no use. A high-pitched scream pierces my palms, followed by a sickening thud. A violent, choking gurgle.

Death smells like salt. It reeks in a way that extends beyond just stench. You feel it in your bones. You taste it: the bitter flavor of someone else's soul escaping on the air. They steal a piece of you along with it.

Though I doubt this murderer has anything left of his to lose.

"I didn't know," Boris says, still eerily calm despite the violence. In fact…I get the sense he enjoyed the gruesome show. "You should pick your accountants more carefully, *Pakhan*," he adds. "But, if the offer still stands, I'll take the girl. Of course, we'll need to send for a new accountant—"

"Get out." Mischa looms in the shadows like a specter. His chest heaves erratically as he callously swipes his knife along his pants to clean it while his gaze roves in my direction. "Leave!" he snarls at Boris. "We'll continue this later. You—" He never takes his eyes off me. The hue of them clashes violently with the red liquid splattered across his chest. Blood reflected in more blood. "*Upstairs.*"

Moving blindly, I make it up the basement stairs in seconds and find my way to the main staircase by feel alone. The darkness distorts my already limited vision. Every shadow morphs into the shape of a man chasing me up the steps and into that narrow bedroom.

Once inside it, I don't close the door. I creep toward the bed instead, intending to sit on the mattress. I miss and wind up on my knees, pressing my bleeding cheek against the cold floor. My stomach roils, but nothing escapes my abused, sore throat. I don't know what's more alarming. The terror I feel? Or how quickly my body is able to process it.

Breathe, Ellen...

I inhale noisily, aware of the blood flooding my mouth for the first time. My nose feels tender to the touch. My right eye aches, impossible to open. I can't tell if the thumping in my ears is my heartbeat or approaching footsteps. Then the light switches on with a hiss, illuminating the puddle of blood growing beneath me.

"How?" Every step Mischa takes echoes, alarmingly unsteady. He's lost that smooth, predatory prowl. All that's left are harsh motion and tension.

Through a tangled net of my hair, I watch him advance. In one hand, he's holding Xavier's briefcase, but the money's been hastily shoved back in, peeking through gaps in the seal.

"How the fuck did you know?"

I don't have the energy to stand. "Robert," I admit to the floor, watching my saliva mingle with scarlet. "He…taught me."

"He taught you to what? Inspect his money?" His harsh laugh proves he doesn't know whether I'm lying or not. Not that it matters. Logic means less to him with every passing second. He craves the rage and chases it with flared nostrils and a trembling fist. But curiosity wins out. "You really expect me to believe that?"

I don't. But again, it doesn't matter. "He only ever talks to me about money," I explain, even though saving my life is futile. I'm tired. Resisting him is too damn hard. Too fucking bloody. I want it to end. "He made a bad deal once. His father nearly killed him. So he taught me to…" The words trail off, broken and worthless. I doubt he even heard me.

He wants to fight. He wants to kill again. He wants to justify whatever hatred has eaten him alive. He can't have that narrative ruined, not even for his own benefit.

But silly me. I nearly forgot the one constant of the world that has yet to prove me wrong: *money*. A man values nothing more.

"You want to make yourself useful?" he wonders in a hollow tone.

I sense his intention even before his shoulder tenses, but I'm too tired to move. He throws the briefcase at me. It bounces painfully off my hip and falls open, spilling its contents over the floor.

"Then count it. Every last fucking bill. If you're off by so much as a cent, I'll gut you and send you to your fucking *husband* in pieces."

He slams the door in his wake so hard that it jerks on its hinges. Loose bills flutter in the air, falling down softly to coat my body like snowfall. I'm tempted to ignore him. To let him kill me when he returns. Give up here and now.

I'm so tired…

But it would never end there. *Nothing* comes between a man and his money.

CHAPTER 10

It takes me hours to capture and count every last bill, but I do so carefully before tucking the final amount away in my mind. The series of numbers sits heavy and out of place there, like some foreign trinket I never sought to add to my collection. One my husband certainly wouldn't approve of. Picturing Robert's scorn, I'd almost prefer physical penetration— at least my new tormentor would have to leave my body eventually.

But this, I will never forget: He carries five hundred and twenty-five thousand dollars on his person. Or at least he *did*. Now, it's all nothing more than pretty paper, considering that few respectable institutions would accept bills quite literally stained with my blood…

Will he punish me? Retaliation would be the least of my worries, however. I've caused so much more than a stranger's death by blowing the whistle on Xavier's deceit. I've lost Mischa his *accountant*, which I assume is not an easy position to fill in his line of business.

And for good reason.

"No motherfucker worth his salt keeps shit written down anymore," Robert used to tell me, his words rushed with paranoia. "No. A smart man hides his secrets where no one would think to look. That's the key, Elle. Somewhere safe."

Like locked inside a woman's head…

Rotting wood creaks nearby, betraying footsteps. Rushed. I stiffen at the realization that someone's standing above me before I can even turn my head in their direction.

"God have mercy…"

The hunched shadow seems familiar. Vanya? Either he teleported to my side or delirium is stealing my consciousness bits at a time. I can't see his face, just a blur lacking any definition, but his voice rings out clearly.

"Sleep," he insists, prying the last bloodied stack of money from my grip. "You're safe… Just sleep."

His voice trembles with the grim truth that he has no way of honoring that promise. Not really, yet he chooses to lie anyway. Out of pity or denial?

I'm not sure.

I'm too tired to really give a damn either way.

***

*P*ain keeps me tethered to my body, pulling me in and out of wakefulness—too strong to ignore for long, but too intense to suffer at the same time. Like a toy ball, I'm bounced between consciousness and delirium, but terror is the tiebreaker.

It scuttles at the edge of my awareness, growing more potent the more I become aware of the scent flooding my lungs—and the voice in my head. Deep. Guttural. Merciless.

"Look at me."

I can't. My eyelids are too heavy to lift. Whenever I try, I only see indistinguishable smears of light and shadow. So I just feel instead. *Pain, pain, pain.* But, beneath it all…relief?

My fingers perform an agonizing journey to my jaw, brushing something stiff and dry secured there. Gauze? Someone must have bandaged the wound on my face again, as well as draped me beneath what feels like cotton. The bedsheets? They're warm against my throbbing skin—which is the only part of my body in any semblance of comfort. My skull is a fragile shell that barely contains my thoughts. They threaten to spill out at any moment, like so much blood already has.

Breathe, Ellen. Breathe…

"Look at me."

All I can do is tilt my head in the general direction of his voice. As if to betray me, my vision slowly returns, and his features come into stark focus before I'm ready. Cold gaze. Harsh expression. He's cleaned the blood from his hands and changed his clothes, at least. His hair hangs freely down his shoulders, contrasting with his hooded, empty eyes.

"You have five hundred and fifteen thousand dollars in real bills," I croak out before he can issue another command. "One hundred bills were fake—ten thousand dollars altogether."

He scowls at the deceit, but his anger lacks the fire it should. He already knew. Maybe he counted the money after I did, using my own tricks for his benefit? Whatever the reason, testing my skills isn't his reason for waking me.

"Get up," he says, proving my instinct correct. "You're coming with me."

My heart hammers a pathetic resistance. *No. No. No.* I'm too tired. I can't do this again. I can't be sold, but I can't fight him, either. My eyelids fall, trapping tears stinging beneath them. "Just kill me."

"When I'm good and ready." Again, his voice lacks any real emotion. Something's tempered his anger, allowing him to hone it, at least for now. "You will come with me. Get up."

My head pulses in torment as I haul myself upright. The room is devoid of anyone else. Judging from the stiffness in my muscles, I've slept for a few hours, maybe longer. An entire day? The blackness beyond the window offers no clues. I have to decipher what I can from the man staring down at me. His knuckles have bruised and my cheek smarts in sympathy. So it *has* been hours, at least. Was Vanya the reason for my long reprieve?

I don't find him lurking in the doorway, and disappointment joins the flood of emotions racking my body. So much for his promise.

"Hurry up," Mischa snaps, already near the door.

I bite back the agony moving inspires in order to stand. The room spins around me, distorted by the fact that I only have the use of one eye. When Mischa heads into the hall, I do my best to follow him, but my body sways unsteadily. Before I can regain my balance, both legs twist beneath my weight, and the floor rushes to meet me.

Only a grip on my shoulder keeps me from crumbling into an unceremonious heap. *Mischa.* Without a word, he pulls me after him, navigating the cramped floor plan.

It's either my imagination or fact, but he moves at a pace I can manage. When I falter, he uses his grip on me to keep me on balance. There's no cruelty in his touch for once. Just strength and a foreboding feeling I can't escape. We don't run into Vanya on our way to a wooden door that opens onto a decrepit porch. Near the steps leading to the ground level, a van is parked. Mischa steers me to it without explanation and climbs into the back seat after me.

This time, our driver is joined by another man who's quietly sporting a gun on his lap. The moment the door closes after us, the van lurches into motion, heading down a gravel road.

I'm not dumb enough to look back at the house we left behind, so I stare at my hands instead, noticing more signs of simple kindness. Someone cleaned the blood from my fingers. They bandaged my foot as well and treated the other open wounds on my neck. It's a show of mercy I'm not used to. Poor Vanya holds enough humanity for two households, and the thought is sadder than anything I've experienced up until this point.

If only he could share part of his soul with the man beside me.

As if sensing the direction my thoughts have taken, Mischa places one of his hands over his right hip, near his blade. A lethal reminder.

"You disobey me here, Little One," he begins harshly, "And—"

"You'll kill me," I finish for him. I don't know where the defiance comes from.

"So, your husband taught you to count his money," Mischa says carefully. When I gather the nerve to look, his expression is unreadable. "Why?"

I consider lying, but the answer spills over my tongue before I can craft a good one. "He said I was the only calculator he could trust." Parroting those words out loud sends a chill down my spine. It feels wrong. Like I've betrayed some secret hidden in Robert's madness. It feels...strange.

"Calculator? Did he have you do this for him often?"

I should lie. "No. Yes." Once again, the truth spills out against my will. My tongue burns, as if every word is poison being expelled from my system. Will I survive without an antidote? Who knows. "He kept an accountant, but—" *Enough.* I bring my hand to my mouth, pressing my lips closed.

Beside me, Mischa stays eerily patient. He waits long enough for me to hope that he'll let it go. "But?"

I don't recognize the sound that trickles from my throat. A groan? A laugh? Whatever it is sounds too distorted to recognize. "*But* you cannot fuck your accountants into submission, can you?"

In my right mind, I'd never say something so vulgar. So cold. In my right mind...

"How many 'numbers' did you keep for him?" Mischa asks. "Do you remember them?"

"N-no." The lie sticks this time, though not for Robert's benefit. "He only ever had me double-check his real accountant."

Does he believe that? I can't tell. Even in the close confines of the back seat, he takes care to avoid any contact between us. If I couldn't see him from my peripheral vision, he could have been light-years away. A distant shadow clawing its way through my past in search of something to feed on.

This time, he lets me huddle in silence for a few minutes longer, and I use the reprieve to gather my scattered senses and lock them up tight. It's the pain that makes me so reckless. My thoughts are harder to string together. My fear of Robert takes more energy to grasp. I need to stay silent. Silent…

But silence here sounds different than it did at Winthorp Manor. There's no fragile peace to be found. Just my racing heartbeat to count the seconds, and the sound of Mischa's knuckles cracking in a menacing fashion.

Then…

"Why do you hate him so much? R-Robert?"

At the sound of my voice, remnants of anger flare, igniting whatever calm he's maintained until now. *Poof!* There's no more eerie patience. "I suggest you focus on yourself, Ellen Winthorp."

I obey, facing straight ahead once again. I'm painfully aware of the fact that he hasn't covered my eyes yet, though I can't make out much of our surroundings beyond the van. Just flickering shadows, broken every now and again by an impenetrable sky.

I'm more than willing to play by his rules: *Shut up.* My teeth clench tight against disobedience.

But he ruins his own game. "You haven't asked to go back to him."

No. I don't like this line of questioning. It's far too dangerous. I turn to the window, but his palm finds my chin, reinforcing the fact that, at any second, he can make me look at him.

"You haven't pleaded," he adds softly. "When that man saw you in the woods, you didn't run. You didn't cry out. I *know* you saw him—"

"I'm of more use to Robert alive than dead," I say.

But that's not it. Once again, he's peered beneath my skin without permission, seeking what lurks below the surface. Secrets I can't name. Horrors I won't face—not again.

"You shouldn't worry about being useful to *him...*" He brings his mouth near my ear. "Most wives are willing to *barter* for their husbands."

Barter? I lick my lips tentatively. "W-what do you want?"

He lets me go and pretends to mull it over. But there's a reason why he brought me along to wherever he's going. One I'm not sure I want to discover in full.

"What I want is simple." He snatches my wrist and presses something against my palm: a stack of bills. "Count."

He doesn't mean by amount. Slowly, I flip through each bill, feeling the paper for imperfections. "They're all real," I deduce once finished.

For whatever reason, he doesn't take the money back just yet. Instead, the trip comes to a sudden stop in darkness. Near darkness, anyway. Faint light betrays the shapes of other vehicles parked nearby. A garage? Distracted by him, I missed any sign of civilization.

Or any hope of escape.

"Come on." Mischa shoulders the door on his end open, while his men wait in the vehicle. Jerking his chin, he indicates for me to follow, but not them.

I shiver as my bare feet hit the icy pavement. We're underground, definitely in some kind of garage. Up ahead, an elevator waits, opening its doors as if on cue the moment we approach. Mischa enters first, pulling me in after him. I sense that unnerving calm once again. He's determined.

To sell me?

I find myself staring down at my fist, desperate for a distraction. I'm still holding his money. At least a grand, maybe more. Is this my going price? My stomach clenches at the thought. Robert always claimed that I was worth diamonds, but what would he give to have me back now? Morbid imagery pops into my head: diamonds drenched in blood.

"Stay close." It's the only warning my captor bothers to issue before the elevator doors part, revealing a long hallway decorated with burgundy wallpaper and rich ebony carpet.

Faint music drifts from a pair of closed doors up ahead, where a man in black is waiting, his expression stoic. When we approach him, the man steps aside.

"*Pakhan*," he greets.

As the doors open, I'm suddenly self-conscious of how I must look: like a prisoner of war being paraded after her captor. I run my free hand halfheartedly through my hair, but it's no use. Blood and bruises can only be obscured by so much.

The room beyond contains at least five people, spread throughout a grand layout that resembles a casino. A luxury bar dominates one wall, while a poker table seats three of the five men. They are wearing suits and sharing a cigar between them. The atmosphere is light and friendly, while the remaining men linger on the periphery, their arms crossed, their eyes straight ahead.

One of the figures at the poker table spots us and rises to his feet. "Mischa! Welcome! Welcome!" He's tall. Maybe forty, with a thinning goatee and piercing, green eyes. Unlike Xavier's imitation, his suit is real and tailored to perfection. As we approach, he reaches out to Mischa and then firmly clasps his hand. "How kind of you to enter my humble abode. It's just a spare room, for me and the boys." He gestures to the two men beside him, and they aren't mirroring his charming grin. They're on edge.

"Nicolai," Mischa says, drawing his hand away. He's wary as well. Tension hardens his posture, disrupting the otherwise calm surface he projects.

"Well…" Nicolai smiles in a chilling display of ivory teeth. "I know you're a busy man, so best to get business out of the way," he says. "Now, tell me again how you cheated me out of *my* money?"

The words have the effect of striking a match near a pool of gasoline.

Whoosh!

"It wasn't intentional." Mischa stiffens and jerks his chin toward me. "My previous accountant made an error. But I have the full amount."

He snatches the wad of bills from me and places them down on the poker table.

Nicolai snaps his fingers and one of the seated men quickly counts the money. "It's all here," the man declares once finished.

"Excellent." As Nicolai claps his hands, his smile returns, but it never reaches his eyes. Chilling and endless, they hone in on me. "And who is this?"

"A new toy of Ivan's," Mischa explains. A lie. But why?

"I see…" Nicolai nods, rubbing his chin. "He always did have a soft spot for his women."

"Her old owner was an accountant," Mischa says, continuing his distortion of the truth. "He taught her to count. She's the one who noticed Xavier's *mistakes*."

"Hmph." Nicolai chuckles in amusement. "I assume he's been shown the error of his ways?"

"Permanently," Mischa declares so viciously that I shiver.

"Excellent." Nicolai clasps his hands together once again. "Now that that nasty business is taken care of, I suppose all that's left is for you to carry out that favor you owe me. For the inconvenience."

A slight narrowing of his eyes is the only clue to Mischa's confusion. "Favor?"

"After all, I've always supplied your family and organization with unwavering loyalty and support," Nicolai continues, still smiling. "You fuck with my money, even by *accident*, and you fuck with a domino chain that extends well beyond the *Mafiya*. My other clients don't like scandal, you see." He shrugs dismissively as if to say, *Can't be helped.* "As retribution for such an error, I will humbly accept whatever help you see fit to bestow, *Pakhan*."

"Of course." A muscle in Mischa's neck twitches, but his voice never loses that low, cautious cadence. "What do you need?"

"Nothing big." Nicolai snaps his fingers a second time and a door near the back of the room opens.

Two people enter, and it's almost like watching a mirror image. A small, ragged figure trails a man nearly twice her size. Her shoulder-length hair makes her childish features seem even larger—enormous brown eyes and a little nose. She's young. Too young. When they reach the poker table, her companion sets a gray duffle in the center and unzips it.

"The finest cocaine," Nicolai declares almost lovingly while eyeing the small, round packets the bag contains. Each one is no larger than a golf ball, rubbery in appearance. "Several uncut grams," he adds, "all ready to be consumed by one of the wealthiest men in the world. This client tends to be tricky to supply, however. He likes it brought to him directly, and let's just say he travels within a…select posse. Tonight, they're at a hotel in the city. I believe you're familiar with the location?"

Mischa nods.

"Excellent. All I need you to do is escort my friend here to the rendezvous. There are clothes for both of you in the bag. Get her through security and leave the cocaine where my client can retrieve it discreetly. Then our debt shall be settled. Oh, and"—Nicolai lifts a packet for inspection—"my new chemist doesn't know his head from his ass. These packets will last only about an hour, tops, in the body, and that's roughly how long it will take to reach my client. So speed will be of the essence. Though, if the girl survives, you can have her." He reaches out, running his fingers through her blond hair. "I'm sure you can find some *use* for her in one of those clubs of yours."

"Where am I meeting this client?" Mischa demands, swatting the suggestion aside.

Nicolai rattles off what sounds like a random number. "Make sure she swallows the cocaine before you arrive. I'm sure there will be a blockade of some sort, searching vehicles. And, if by some bad turn of luck, you *do* get caught…"

"We were never here," Mischa says. Turning to the girl, he snatches up the duffle. "Come on."

In utter silence, she follows us back to the elevator and into the garage, where the van is still idling, ready to pull away the moment we climb into the back seat.

As the door slams shut, Mischa forms a fist and punches the window. "Damn it!"

Sandwiched between us, the girl doesn't react to the outburst, but I flinch. I can't take my eyes off the duffle. I can't stop hearing Nicolai's words echo in my head. *If the girl survives, you can keep her.*

Even the Winthorps weren't so callous when it came to human life. They killed their toys quickly, and when they were no longer of any use.

And, despite his own brand of cruelty, something tells me that even Mischa is balking at the logistics of this plan. Smuggling drugs in the body of a child so that some rich bastard can get his fix. I *almost* believe it.

Until I see his face. He's lost that fragile calm again. In its absence, darkness consumes all that's left. Poor Vanya was wrong: There's nothing human about this creature. Without a word of explanation, he unzips the duffle and rummages through it for a bottle of water, which he shoves aside. Then a packet he hands to the girl. "Put this in your—"

"No." My hand flies out before I can stop it, gripping his forearm. *No!* Some frantic voice at the back of my mind sounds a meaningless warning. But it's too faint to hear clearly. *Don't do this, Ellen…*

As if used to a routine, the girl obediently grabs the water bottle and tips it toward her mouth, but I snatch it away before she can even down a drop.

"Don't." Reaching across her, Mischa snatches my wrist. "Stay the fuck out of this."

My sore body throbs at the warning in his tone. Disobeying him is futile. I know that, but I hold my free hand out anyway.

"Give it to me," I demand, nodding toward the packet.

Words can't describe how rage distorts his features. His fingers clench, but if he hits me in such a narrow space, the girl will be caught in the middle.

Lunging toward him, I snatch a packet from the bag and shove it into my mouth. Only sheer force of will can override the instinct to spit it right back out. *Swallow, swallow!* My gag reflex triggers. Even the water doesn't help. I have to *shove* the packet down with shaking fingers, igniting my already tender throat in the process.

"Fuck!" A heavy hand swipes at my mouth in vain.

"It's too late," I somehow manage to croak as my throat struggles to down the foreign object. "I already swallowed it. Now, give me the rest before…"

Before time runs out.

CHAPTER 11

$\mathcal{I}$ barely fit the dress meant for the girl—it's too damn big. Made of white cotton, its modest neckline is more conservative than anything else I've worn over the past few days. But that's about the only improvement.

The tailored suit Nicolai provided fits Mischa perfectly, however. *Unfairly.* With his hair slicked away from his face, he could almost pass for another person. Some rich, cold businessman with enough money to hide whatever secrets his scars might reveal.

In the right lighting, he could even pass for a Winthorp.

The only flaw in his ruse is that he drives himself rather than commands a chauffeur, as Robert would. After we changed, he left the girl with his two companions a few streets away from the rendezvous point. They were to call someone from the safe house and then Mischa would return later. If...

Well, I suppose that depends on how quickly my body digests the thin layer of material encasing the cocaine. An hour, Nicolai said.

Twenty minutes have passed already.

"You fucking idiot." They're the only three words Mischa has said to me since pulling off. "Do you have any idea what the hell you've done? I should kill you. I'll fucking make you suffer—"

"Like that girl would have suffered?" *Oh, God.* The vitriolic response spilled out of me before I could choke it down. Though I doubt there's any room left in my stomach for more suppression. More lies. More fear. So, for once, I forget my mantra. I don't breathe. I yell. "She's a child!"

"Is that so?" He laughs darkly while manipulating the steering wheel, cutting off an oncoming vehicle, the driver of which honks his displeasure. "You don't know a fucking thing about that *child*. You think she hasn't done it before?"

Because she has. Scars haunted her eyes, deeper and more violent than anything found on my skin. Scars like the ones haunting the boy who intruded into Briar's room all those years ago. Though their circumstances may be different, they both had no choice in the matter.

"So that makes it right?" I question. "Even Robert wouldn't—"

"Don't." With one hand, he grips the back of my neck in warning. "You don't know a fucking thing about what your Winthorp is capable of."

"He never cut my face," I counter, glaring through blurred vision. I couldn't hold my tears back if I tried. So I don't. I let them fall. "*He* never put me in a cage, and he's done...terrible, terrible things. But even he would *never*—"

"You think you know me enough to compare me to him?"

The vehicle slows to a stop. We're on a narrow street where lights flicker nearby. Flashlights? At first, I think he's stopped to threaten me, wasting precious time. But then a beam of light shines directly through the windshield.

"Shit."

Mischa lets me go, and I hunch over, hiding my face. It's the one little detail I didn't consider before sacrificing myself. The girl was clean and whole enough to play a role in Nicolai's charade without catching notice. Even Mischa excels at playing pretend. As an officer approaches his side of the car, he sits taller and lowers his window, resembling the guest of some important gala. Only I can see the gun tucked beneath his seat.

"Good evening," he greets while I observe his every move through the curtain of my hair.

"Where are you headed?" The unfamiliar voice belongs to the officer.

"We just came back from the opera," Mischa says, nodding toward me. "She fell asleep halfway and demanded we return to the hotel."

He chuckles warmly while the officer peers in my direction. "Oh? Can I see your ID and registration please?"

Mischa hands the documents over and precious seconds pass while the officer scrutinizes each one. Finally... He steps back and beckons us forward with a wave of his hand. "Move along."

As the officer passes by, Mischa visibly deflates. He's more cautious than nervous. Like he accused of the girl, he's done this before. Just how many times? With *how* many women, their bellies stuffed with drugs? I'm almost tempted to ask him, but then I notice the time on the dashboard.

There isn't much left.

To compound matters, Nicolai vastly understated the "exclusive company" his client must keep. Police cars are lurking near the front of the hotel when we draw closer, their lights turned off as officers scour those entering and leaving the elegant building.

"Shit." Rather than circle for the valet, Mischa takes a shortcut toward the employee entrance. He knows the way, parking in an empty, secluded space beside a dumpster.

I exit the van after him and realize, even before I see his jaw clench in frustration, that there's no way in hell we can go through the main security. Parking alone cost us three minutes.

There're barely twenty left.

"This way. Keep your head down." He takes my wrist and drags me across the parking lot and then through an emergency exit that opens into a laundry room of some kind. By some oversight, there's no security here—yet, anyway—and Mischa moves swiftly, navigating a maze of rooms and industrial-sized machinery.

Twenty minutes.

Nineteen.

I stop counting.

Past the laundry room, we take a service elevator that brings us to the main lobby of the hotel, but rather than head out in the open, Mischa shoves me into a stairwell. We climb two flights in seconds. Then five more. Ten. Twenty. Thirty.

I'm panting, dripping sweat, by the time he finally stops at a floor. My stomach hurts. *Don't think about it,* I try to tell myself. But running aids digestion, doesn't it?

How many minutes? I can't remember…

"In here."

We reach a hallway of closed doors, but he passes them all, heading right to one at the end. A potted plant rests beside the door. Crouching, Mischa rakes his fingers through the dirt and withdraws a keycard from the base of the plant before I can question. On the first swipe, the reader flashes red. No good. On the second attempt…

Green!

The door opens to a spacious suite. It's impressive, decorated in black leather and white accents, but I only have eyes for the bathroom. I race to the sink. Bent over it, I open my mouth and try to gag. Nothing. I cram a finger down my throat, but it's not enough.

"Move!" He shoves my hands aside, and three thick fingers trigger my gag reflex, causing my stomach to erupt in protest.

One bag comes up, still intact. Another. Another…

"That's ten," Mischa grunts after what feels like an eternity. "Five more."

His fingers continue to assault my esophagus, but minutes tick by without another packet. Too long.

"Shit."

He shoves me toward the tub. Before I can get my bearings, his hands form fists over my stomach, and with a grunt, he thrusts them both. Hard. One packet comes up. Another.

"Keep going! One more."

"I can't…" Horror steals the words from my throat. It's too late. The last packet's already dissolved. I know it has. Any second, I'll go into shock. Die. *Stupid, Ellen. Stupid—*

"Don't think about anything else," Mischa snarls, gripping me tight. "Just fucking *breathe.* Do it!"

Harsh fingers ram into my stomach. Again. Again.

"Ugh!" I double over and bring up the last packet, shaking with exertion.

He drops me there, slumped over the tub. I'm only conscious enough to hear him run some water, cleaning the acid from the packets before tucking them away. I can't move. I can't think.

I just breathe, fighting for air as the bathroom fades. I'm a child again, back in Winthorp Manor.

Something was wrong.

From the hallway, I heard footsteps. My mother's? But no. These were too heavy, and the figure appearing in my doorway was far too large. His blond hair peeked from the edge of a black woolen cap. The color that made my heart stop. He was wearing it from head to toe: black slacks and a dark sweatshirt meant to disguise him in the shadows.

The second he met my gaze, I knew. He was dangerous, just like the men my mother warned me to avoid. Something silver glinted in his hand. A blade.

He pointed it at me, his jaw clenched. But his hand wavered. His eyes were too wide. Fearful?

Suddenly, he pointed to the bed.

"Get under it," he warned. "Don't think. Don't move. You just fucking breathe."

Trembling and terrified, I had no choice but to obey, crawling on my stomach beneath Briar's silk sheets. I'd only just tucked my legs beneath the frame when I heard the soft thud of another stranger's approach—someone who sounded way too big to be a regular maid.

"Is she in here?" another man demanded, his voice thick. Guttural. He talked as strangely as the boy did, betraying a heavy accent. "Well, is she?"

"I don't know," the younger man replied as I inhaled raggedly, obeying his command. Breathe. Breathe. Breathe! *"But we should leave. Now. Before they return."*

They? Robert and his father. There was a gala that night. That's why Robert was wearing a suit earlier that day. It was his first time attending the grown-up parties.

"Leave?" the older man hissed. My stomach churned as thuds resonated through the floor: footsteps inching farther into the room. "You don't make the shots, boy. Check. She has to be here."

"I've looked." Lighter footfalls drift toward the opposite end of the room. "She's not here. We should be looking for Anna—"

"We are," the older man insisted, his tone harsh. "But I will not let this insult stand. I don't care if she's just a child. The little whelp will pay for her father's sins—"

"Did you hear that?" the younger boy interjected. "Someone's coming. We need to move!"

Silently, they crept back into the hall, but I couldn't move. Not even when my bladder protested and warm liquid dripped down my legs. Not even when a soft, small hand slipped beneath the mattress runner and brushed my wrist.

"Ellen?" Briar's face appeared through the darkness next, inches from mine. "Are you okay?" she asked, her eyes wide.

Only later would I learn that she heard the boy coming way before I had. Thinking quickly, she'd hidden in the closet.

Leaving me behind…

"Drink." Something cool brushes my cheek. "Drink!"

I blink as the rim of a water bottle presses against my mouth, but I shake my head. I doubt I'll be able to swallow ever again.

"No." For whatever reason, Mischa won't let me turn away. He grips my chin and grinds the rim of the bottle against my teeth. "Fucking *drink*."

I cringe with the first sip, surprised when it goes down with less pain than expected. Before I know it, I've drained the entire bottle.

And all that's left to do is face the wrath awaiting me.

"It was you," I croak, watching Mischa scowl at the confession from the corner of my eye. His gaze darts toward the sink as if counting the packets to ensure I really did expel them all.

But I'm not delirious. For the first time in so long, I see everything clearly.

"You were the boy," I add. "In Winthorp Manor. I saw you. You thought I was Briar."

Yet he saved *me*.

His eyes widen and narrow in quick succession. Remembering? Or suppressing. Gritting his teeth, he shakes his head, dismissing the accusation. "You dumb bitch," he hisses, tightening his grip on my shoulder. "I should kill you—"

"Better me than a child," I whisper. Vanya was right. Mischa wasn't always this way—but that knowledge only makes his fall all the more tragic. "I'd rather die than let you use her."

"Oh?" he laughs. "You stupid bitch. I wouldn't have made her *swallow* it."

Too breathless to speak, I stiffen at the confession, my eyes wide. There's a grim honesty to his words. Even I can't deny it.

"I know this fucking hotel," he adds. "All she had to do was hide them in the dress—"

"You'd still…use…a child as a pawn." It hurts to speak. My voice grates over the air, pathetic and broken.

He hears me regardless. Radiating hatred, his body cages mine from behind, trapping me against the tub and tile flooring. There's nowhere to run—not that I have the energy. I just press my bruised cheek against the rim and wait.

If silence alone were as far as his cruelty went, I could survive it. But no. His touch creeps along my injured cheek, aggravating the sore flesh.

I have no choice but to beg. "If you're going to kill me, just kill me."

"Kill you?" He growls out a terrifying imitation of a laugh against my shoulder. "I should. It would be fucking easier than keeping you alive."

He's still touching me. Rough fingers swipe at my cheek—to test the bandage, I realize. Next, he grabs my ankle to ensure the one on my foot is intact. There's a rehearsed familiarity to the motions. Almost as if…

"You cleaned me." My voice echoes off the basin of the tub, hollow with shock. "*You* bandaged me—"

"But maybe I *should* kill you," he counters, ignoring my accusation. All at once, his hands fall away. "Is that what your fucking Winthorp would do? *You* compared me to the bastard, so tell me how this ends. With you dead?"

I shake my head without bothering to reply out loud. Robert would never kill me. That would require that he give me something I actually want.

An escape.

"Then what?" Mischa wonders coldly. His fingers return to rake through my hair, softer than before. Alarm bells go off in my mind. Once again, he proves to be unpredictable. Wild. Dangerous. "You compared *me* to *him*," he reminds me, hissing into my ear. "So fucking tell me what I'm supposed to do next."

I tremble at the implications of such a question. What would Robert do? He'd play a game, of course. One of his favorites.

"He'd kiss me," I hear myself croak, naming the first stage of any twisted session. "He'd touch me. Make me beg…"

"Beg him for what?" His voice is too raw, scorching my tender skin. Anger on him is like wildfire; within the blink of an eye, it's too violent to be contained. "Don't feign you're mute now." He cups my sore throat from behind, sliding his fingers along my windpipe in a chilling caress, daring me to lie to him. "He'd make you beg him for what?"

The memories chase me. Haunt me.

"To stop…"

"He'd hurt you?"

My nerves cringe at the genuine curiosity in his tone as he hooks a hand beneath my waist and flips me onto my back with my head propped against the rim of the tub.

But I don't scream.

He's too heavy. His eyes are empty, the gaze of a monster. But his mouth…

Crushed to mine with no warning, there's no comparison. Robert bites, and licks, and takes. But Mischa just claims. His lips are too soft. Not possessive and unfeeling—but *fire*. There's no teasing buildup. No savoring of my fear. He slides his tongue between my lips and just steals what he wants. With hard, searing thrusts. With heat. With more fire.

He destroys every instinct before I can remember what emotions to salvage. In the resulting chaos, all I can do is feel. Everything.

"He touched you?" Mischa growls against my parted lips, remembering the second stage.

"Y-yes…"

With deft motions, he unhooks the back of my dress. His fingers still against my spine as if waiting for me to react. Scream. Run. When I don't, his fingers drift lower and my body quakes at the feel of his warm flesh molded over solid muscle.

"And then," he snarls into my open mouth. "What?"

I beg. Always. Without fail. Robert never heeds my pleas, but they come anyway. It's our tradition. My torment. His game.

My lips flutter, ready to play, but Misha takes his role of my husband too seriously. His hand descends between us, unzipping his pants to an erection straining against his boxers. His fingers capture mine, forcing me beneath the waistband to feel him for myself. Hot. Silken. Steel.

"Go on," he goads, bucking into my fist, testing my grip. "Beg."

Stop. He's bigger than Robert. He'll hurt me more than my husband ever could. I know it. I feel it. I…

Breathe, Ellen. Breathe. Breathe. Breathe!

"Come on." Frowning, Mischa meets my gaze directly, still throbbing against my fingers. "Play your part, Little One," he commands. "Beg me to stop."

My lips flutter, but when I say nothing, he laughs, throwing his head back.

"You can't take me. Admit it. I am nothing like him. I'll fucking *break* you."

It's a promise. One that adds a new level of danger I've never felt before to the game. No one has ever taken *anything* from Robert Winthorp.

Nothing.

I'm so sure of that that I can't stop myself from croaking, "Will you?"

I almost sound amused. Intrigued?

At the prospect, my captor growls in irritation, freeing himself from his boxers. To prove that he can. That he will. And as I stare down at what rises beneath a thatch of blond curls, a word comes to mind. Something terrifying. A term I'd never apply, even to Robert.

Beautiful?

Dusky flesh and glistening ridges form a cock as repulsive as it is impressive. He could break me.

And maybe there will be nothing left...

"Beg." He hammers the word into my skin with his teeth, nipping the flesh of my throat. He's too close. Flexing his hips brings him between my legs. Heavy. Dominating.

A moan dies behind my teeth as the slick crown of his cock bats against my entrance. Beg? But how? I can't get any air to go into my lungs.

Robert would take his time at this point in the game, stretching me with his fingers, telling me all the while that I want him. *We were made for each other, Elle,* he'd croon.

There is no such teasing with Mischa.

"Fine, Little One," he snarls, bracing his hand against my thigh. "I'll show you just how much like him I can be." One flex of his hips and he slams into me with a groan. A curse. A million fucking words hissed in English and whatever language he natively speaks.

I see black. Then white porcelain as my head falls back and a scream claws its way from my throat. He's too fucking big. I'm too tight. We just *don't* fit, and that natural deterrent demands one solution: He has to force his way into me. Thrust after thrust. Over. Over. Again.

I feel him in my skull, like a battering ram, fucking my body and not just the space between my legs. All of me.

"Say it," he grits out between clenched teeth. "Fucking…say it. I'll stop—"

An answering moan trickles from my lips. I can't contain it. Begging, finally?

But no. My ears catch my own voice whispering something far more dangerous. "M-more." I tremble, every nerve in an uproar.

This isn't part of the script. This isn't right. This isn't…Robert.

He's not Robert.

That fact is only solidified by how roughly he thrusts into me— not patient and unhurried. He's *frenzied.* Splitting me open. Ripping me apart.

Like he doesn't *need* to save me for another round. I'm not his toy to keep unbroken.

"What…what the fuck did you say?" he demands. But his body contradicts the anger in his voice. Even now, he's throbbing and thickening. So deep. Not deep enough. "Stop." Gritting his teeth, he starts to withdraw, hissing into my ear, "Tell me to stop." It's not a command as much as it is a plea.

But there are no rules anymore. My body has a mind of its own, taking control of my throat to voice it as my knees draw up around him. "M-more—"

"Fuck," he hisses in confusion, gripping my hips.

Before I can even register his absence, he's back. Deeper. Harder. Faster. Our lips fuse, grappling for leverage, and I finally feel the fear I should. It's hotter than fire. Than hate. Burning. Scorching. Desolating.

"Beg," he pleads, still on a vicious race toward his own release.

But my lips seal shut as a grim realization sinks in: *I won't beg…*

I don't want to.

It's like that single thought is the trigger to surrender. My body tightens, rippling around him, collapsing in on itself. He snarls at the reaction, still thrusting. Harder. Faster.

He fucks his rage into me without mercy. Everything. I feel him shuddering with release and sullying the shell of Robert Winthorp's "whore." Deflated, he slumps against me, knocking the air from my chest.

And I lie here, letting him crush me.

CHAPTER 12

I hover on the edge of consciousness for what feels like an eternity. Any minute, I'm sure someone will kick, shake, or threaten me awake—but that moment never comes.

I'm left alone to suffer, and in the end, hunger is what finally rouses me. My stomach aches. So does my head. Between my legs… *No.* I ignore that pain and focus only on what I can fix now. *Food.*

Gradually, my eyes open to an unfamiliar ceiling and unease returns. I don't recognize the bed I'm lying on; it's too soft to be the one in the safe house. The sheets twisted around me feel clean, but the comfort they impart doesn't do much to negate the terrifying reality that someone stripped me naked. That *everything* hurts. The insides of my legs feel sticky…used.

Don't think about that, Ellen.

Groaning, I roll onto my side, trying to find a semblance of familiarity in the darkness. I track the twisting shadows and vague furniture-like shapes without recognizing much. There's too much space. I cradle my forehead against my palm and try to remember. *Hotel room.* Mischa must have kept me here. *Left* me here? I don't sense him nearby.

When I finally crawl from the bed, drawing a white sheet around me, he doesn't lunge from the corner and command me to stay. In fact, there doesn't appear to be anyone else in the suite but me. Beyond the bedroom is a small sitting area and then the bathroom. Someone left the light on in the latter area. The floor looks wet, scrubbed down. A chemical odor itches my nostrils.

Rather than inspect further, I aim for the mini fridge in the corner, tucked into a tiny alcove. Whoever bought this room must have paid for the complimentary mini bar in advance. It's already been stocked, and I grab a pack of crackers and a soda. The pain in my throat is enough to temper my hunger, however. I can only choke a few crumbs down at a time, and even hearing the soda hiss as I pop the top makes me set it aside. Instead, I hunch over the tiny sink above the bar and swap intervals of chewing with measured sips of water from the tap.

That's how he finds me: with my mouth upturned beneath the faucet and the last wet crumbs of cracker clinging to my fingers. I hear his approach rather than see it. His footsteps resonate in slow, steady waves. One step. Another. Pause. Another. Then something lands at my feet, startling me into spraying water down my front.

"Get dressed." Mischa's calm is a distant memory. *Now*, his voice is unsteady. His breathing… Only the thinnest thread of control seems to hold him together.

I sense it wavering the longer I stay hunched over the sink. Slowly, I shut the water off and gather enough nerve to face him.

It's a bad idea. His silhouette flung against the wall is more than enough for me to realize my stupidity for challenging him in the first place. His fingers flex at his sides. Opening and closing. Finally, his shadow flickers and fades as his footsteps head toward the bedroom.

When I crane my neck to look down, I find a pile of fabric at my feet. Clothing. The small white shirt and jeans are all he brought, but I gratefully accept them. Even in my hands, they feel better than a flimsy negligee.

From this position, I can't see the bedroom—or into it—as long as I don't turn around, so I muster what little bravery I have to creep into the bathroom and shut the door. My first action is to run the shower as hot as I can stand it. Then I climb in. *God.* It feels…

Like heaven. Like hell.

Blood and grime wash away from me to circle the drain, but the heat makes everything sting and throb at full force. Every bruise. Every cut. Every brutal "love bite" scraped into the flesh at the nape of my neck.

I feel them all no matter how much I scrub. Clean. Cleanse. Soap and water can't erase him. The soft wash rags the hotel supplies aren't anywhere near strong enough to peel back tainted flesh. Not like the ones at Winthorp Manor, anyway. Those long, hot showers could make me feel new again. Strong again. Afterward, I could always face Robert *again*.

But the longer I stay beneath the scalding spray, the more I'm sure of one chilling truth: I can't ever leave this room. I can't face Mischa. There won't be much left of me to clean if I do.

I think I hide for hours, searching for a state of mind I know I'll never find. My fingers feel bloated, the skin pruned to the point that I can't hold the cloth anymore. It lands at my feet, stuck to the bottom of the tub like something used that can only be scraped off. I'm not sure how long I can last when the door rattles on its hinges.

"Open."

This isn't fair. Even Robert let me escape him for at least a day or two at a time. He gave me that much.

Mischa has no mercy. No fucking soul. When I don't open the door myself, he slides it aside on his own. Dominating the doorway, he's a specter decipherable only in pieces snuck from behind the curtain of my wet hair.

He changed, swapping the suit for his usual fatigues. His hair hangs loose and wild around his shoulders and a sudden memory leaves me trembling: feeling that softness for myself as my fingers gripped his shoulders. Grabbing. Pulling. I stare down in horror at the hands in question, sticky with soap, forever unclean.

"Come," Mischa commands, his voice grated and low. "We need to move. Now."

His tone spurs me into action. I switch the water off and pull my new clothing on without bothering to towel off. He watches me, his gaze searing my bare shoulders while I drag the jeans up over my hips and shimmy into the shirt. They're both too big. I have to roll the pant legs up twice and tuck the shirt in to find some semblance of comfort. By the time I turn to the doorway, he's already entering the hallway.

I follow him and watch as he returns the keycard to the base of the potted plant. It's a quick, silent trip back out to the van, and we leave the hotel behind just as night falls.

Locked in the confines of the vehicle with him, I can't breathe. It's too close. Too quiet. Too dark. My face burns as I remember his cruelty…but my body remembers something different entirely. *Thick, heavy, hot, wet, raw.* Those adjectives trickle across my brain, explicit and vulgar. Robert was firm. Robert was familiar. He never made me say the wrong thing.

More.

My fingers fly up to my lips as if to capture whatever insane impulse made me utter that word. What did I want? More pain? More hate? *No.* The answer lingers in my mind, resisting all attempts to forget: hooded, terrifying eyes. A voice like thunder growled into my ear. More *him.* The living, breathing antidote to my husband. Someone more twisted, and broken, and fucked than Robert could ever be.

My only comfort is that any longer with Mischa and there won't be anything left of me for Robert to reclaim.

"Tell me something. You were more than just his wife." He hisses the words out and veers the van suddenly to the right. "Weren't you? Maybe you fucking planned it, huh? He let me take you? To get inside my fucking head. Is that it?" he demands.

"W-what?" I shake my head. God, the things he's saying. He sounds insane. "What are you talking about—"

"This!" He takes a hand off the wheel and jabs the fingers in my direction. "You're a whore. A snake. From the first fucking second I took you, I knew something was wrong. And now you say you remember me?" He laughs bitterly at the idea. "There's no way in hell he'd let you go. Not without a reason."

Fear renders me silent as the gauge on the dashboard slowly ticks up, up, up. The engine revs as if echoing the way its master speaks.

"Admit it," he snarls. "You aim to seduce me? You really think you can?"

Seduce? Shock overrides every survival instinct warning me to stay silent. "No—"

"No?"

The van comes to a violent stop, which flings me forward against the console. My ears ring. A door opens and slams. Footsteps crunch over gravel, circling over to my side. Cold air rushes in as my door is opened and I'm dragged out onto the side of the road.

"Tell me he sent you," Mischa demands, wrenching me around to face him. "Admit it."

I stumble for balance, forced to confront a terrifying reality. If Robert did plan anything, I'd have been the last to know.

"He didn't," I insist, more to myself than the man beside me. "I swear. He didn't."

Something ugly flashes in Mischa's gaze. He turns, dragging me along with him. *Wham!* Heavy hands slam me against the side of the van and pin me there without mercy. They tug at my jeans, wrenching them down. Then he shoves a fist between my legs, roughly spreading me open around the width of his thumb.

I groan, flinching in surprise.

He hisses. "Fuck. If this isn't a game, then why are you so fucking wet?"

Pressed against cold metal and glass, I say nothing.

Wet. That word means nothing to me. To him, it sounds like a curse, explaining how easily his fingers navigate my flesh without arousing the pain of Robert's groping.

He feels…different. Too raw. Too real. My legs spread without permission, allowing him more access as his snarled insult echoes in my mind. *Whore.*

"Jesus Christ, he *had* to send you," Mischa mutters, sounding crazed. His fingers curl against me, stroking the flesh still sore from his last assault. "But I won't fall for your fucking scheme. Be a good wife, now. Tell me to stop."

Stop. My lips flutter, struggling to form the words. "I…"

"Say it."

I sense him shift as a dangerous rasp echoes. His zipper? Yes. The second the hum trails off, his weight slams into me from behind. Then *he* slams into me, replacing his thumb.

My lips part around a single gasp. It's nearly impossible to describe the sensation of him—massive.

He's in too deep. Deeper than anyone has ever reached, scraping me hollow and shoving himself into crevices even Robert left untouched. My inner muscles clench, desperate to register the intrusion. In or out? Nerves ignite. Flesh tightens, clamping down, drawing him in. In. In. In.

All at once, my throat remembers how to make words. "Oh…*God*—"

"Fuck!" He throws his weight into me.

I see black. Can't feel. Can't breathe. Every sense turns inward, riveted by the sensation of his cock. Twitching inside me. Filling me. Breaking me.

Enraged, he roars. Thrusts. Brutalizes. "Tell me to fucking *stop*."

"More…" It's not the word he wants to hear.

"No!" He grabs my throat from behind, grinding my face against the window, still thrusting. Grunts rip from him with each pass of his hips, each more unsteady than the last. Gritted. Grated. Gasping. "Tell me to stop."

My head is spinning. My body is on fire. Unbearable pressure gathers in my abdomen. Am I suffocating? *You're dying.*

"Fuck!" He bucks into me, twisting his fingers through my hair, grasping, pulling. He's afraid of something. I hear it in his voice. I feel it in how he trembles. His hand leaves my throat and plunges between my legs, pressing into the flesh that surrounds him as if he can stave off whatever I feel building there, gathering in intensity. "Don't you fucking dare."

Too late. The pressure builds and then spills over. It's like a dam breaking: unwelcome, consuming pleasure flooding every fucking pore, crashing through parts of me I kept safe from even Robert. Too much. Not enough. My head rears back against his shoulder as my eyes widen to a mocking view of the endless night sky. God, that's how he feels. *Endless.*

Pain rips through my shoulder: his teeth sinking deep, even as he spits words out against my skin. "You goddamn bitch."

He's furious, but I don't know why. *He's* not the one boneless and senseless, held up only by the weight of his body crushing me to the van. He's not the one with nerves so stimulated that it *hurts*. My nails scrape the window glass, desperate for leverage, but I find nothing. Just cold night air and the taste of a stranger's musk on my tongue.

Still thrusting, he commands me in a twisted language of curses and grunts. "Prove you're not his. Scream for *me*."

I do. Long and loud, without a damn given for who might hear me. I scream until the sound breaks off and air just wheezes from my lungs. Only now does he come, howling his release into my hair. Biting me. Digging in with his nails. The pain keeps me grounded. It makes it harder to ignore what's happening. Harder to forget. Harder to survive.

With one more jagged pass of his hips, he *kills* me. Ellen Winthorp is no more, and there's no one around to mourn her demise. Left behind is a hollow shell that falls to her knees in the dirt while her murderer looms above, wrestling his cock back into his pants.

Limp, I collapse against the cool earth, tears seeping from my eyes as my chest heaves. I'm sobbing in a way I haven't...ever. Not after my mother died. Not after Robert made me his. Not after a madman mistook me for the sister who betrayed me.

Nothing has shattered me like this: his seed seeping out of me and his scent on my skin. Curled into myself, I howl, and I cry, and I *bleed.*

"Get up." He nudges me with his foot when I don't move. "Get the fuck up!"

I don't. So he lifts me himself, hefting me by my shoulders with my legs dragging over the ground. He doesn't return me to my seat. Instead, he moves to the back of the van and opens the trunk. It's connected to the back seat, with a view from the rear windshield. Hiding or terrifying me isn't his goal by shoving me onto the ledge and slamming the lid over me.

This way, I'm out of his sight. Only my mewled, smothered cries give me away as he returns to the front seat and continues to drive.

CHAPTER 13

The van comes to a sudden stop. It's too dark to get my bearings. I have no choice but to wait for the next phase of this ordeal in darkness.

My only coherent thought is to pull my pants up and refasten the zipper before the hood of the trunk raises and night air floods in. Blinking back moonlight, I can only make out a man's general shape looming above me, rigid and shrouded in shadow. Mischa.

He says nothing as I huddle beneath his scrutiny. Instead, he turns away, his footsteps heavy and grated over an uneven surface. Gravel, I see once I lift my head. It paves a makeshift driveway stretching toward a weathered, two-story farmhouse a few yards away. It isn't until I climb out of the van and approach the structure that I realize it's the safe house—and that Mischa never covered my eyes this time. Why? A part of me hesitantly ventures an answer.

Because he knows I won't be leaving. Alive, anyway.

Heavy with dread, I linger at the mouth of the doorway as my vision adjusts to the darkness. He's paces ahead of me, and when he disappears down the hallway, I choose to follow him, finding my way through feel. Disorientation isn't the only reason I cling to the wall for balance. I'm limping. Even Robert never left me so sore after one of his sessions. My legs shake, incapable of supporting my weight.

Breathe, Ellen.

Hushed voices drift from a nearby doorway, giving me some context as to where to go.

"I'm surprised he didn't demand that fucker's head on a platter," a man says. Vanya? "Either way, it was smart to appease him. You can't risk any more enemies. Not while we're out in the open like this."

"Even Nicolai wouldn't dare challenge me," a gruffer voice replies. "He knows who he owes his empire to."

All conversation ceases the moment I reach the doorway. As it turns out, Vanya was the owner of the first voice. I spot him crouched in a corner, cleaning the parts of his gun. One look at me and the color drains from his face while round pieces of metal clatter from his lap to the floor.

"What the hell?"

I should move. I try to, but my legs don't bend correctly. Before I hit the ground, someone grabs me, wrapping their arm around my waist. Vanya? No…

He's in front of me, gazing on with horror as I'm lowered to the ground. "Mischa… *Mal'chik,* what have you done?" The fear in his voice wasn't there before, not even when he warned me of what his leader was capable of. *He won't fuck you, but he will hit you.*

"I'm done lurking in the country like a fucking animal," Mischa says, continuing the thread of whatever conversation I interrupted. He sounds distant, as if he's walking away, leaving me on the floor. "Tomorrow, we come out of hiding. We're going home."

A door slams shut, rattling the floorboards, and I know without even having to look that he's gone. I can breathe again, noisily and labored.

"Fuck." Vanya crouches beside me, swiping my hair from my wounded cheek. Agony alights his gaze: a pain I've never witnessed on anyone before—I've only ever felt it. That horrible feeling that someone you love might have done the unthinkable. Betrayal. "Did he…did he hurt you?" he asks softly.

He's not referring to physically. Somehow, he's been able to rationalize that difference to himself. His Mischa may hit and abuse others, but violate them? That would cross a line even he can't fathom.

Slowly, I shake my head. It's the truth. Mischa hasn't hurt me. He's decimated me.

And you wanted him to…

Vanya clenches his jaw, biting back a question he can't voice. Instead, he rolls me onto my side and covers me with a jacket shrugged from his shoulders. "I'll bring you food," he tells me as I give in to exhaustion. "Get some sleep…"

*F*or the second time in a row, I awake on my own. A hazy, dreamlike daze coats everything in a fog. As I blink up at a peeling ceiling, I almost don't remember. Where I am. What I've done.

I almost forget…

But then an undeniably masculine scent slams into me, ripping away the ignorance. I feel him, even before I see him towering above me.

"Get up."

I comply, maneuvering my sore limbs just enough to rise onto my knees. Vanya's jacket pools on the floor beside me, but I know better than to reach for it, even as my teeth chatter. I'm shocked to find a bottle of water and a sandwich on the floor as well, a few feet away. He kept his promise.

"Eat." Mischa jerks his chin toward the food.

I don't wait for a more explicit invitation. I cram the sandwich into my mouth and barely take a sip of water when he turns for the door.

"Come."

I stagger, an uncoordinated heap. After I nearly run into a wall, he snatches my arm and manually steers me into the hall and out of the house. Outside, a strip of orange accents an otherwise dark sky. Sunset.

Once again, I've slept for an entire day. During that time, Mischa and his men have been busy. There are four vans gathered out front. The men move freely between them, packing materials. In one, a familiar face watches mutely from behind the glass and my heart aches. Small. Round. The girl.

Mischa kept her alive—for now.

"Look at the ground," the man in question hisses.

I obey, allowing him to shove me toward one of the vans and inside it. I expect him to leave, but no. He climbs in after me, this time smothering any space that might separate us. His shoulder deliberately presses against mine, his thigh searing my hip.

As the door closes, his voice trickles down my spine, low and dangerous. "Did you think I'd let you stay near Vanya so that you could feed him more lies?" He rakes his fingers through my hair, unconcerned when they catch on tangles, making me wince. "What did you tell him?"

"N-nothing." I breathe the truth against the window nearest me. Beyond it lies a lonely landscape of naked trees swaying in the darkness. The moon shows full and round—like his thumb blazing a trail across my shoulder and down, igniting a path through the cotton of my shirt.

My chest tightens as the air thickens in my lungs. *Breathe, Ellen.* But I can't. He's in my head as much as he's beside me. Taunting. Teasing.

Destroying.

"Did you tell him that you threw yourself at me like a goddamn whore?" he snarls, his voice low for my benefit.

The driver doesn't react. Not even as his leader's hand creeps...

I stiffen as his thumb grazes the clasp of my jeans. A slow, ruthless tugging undoes my zipper, link by goddamn link.

Without panties as a barrier, his nail grazes my curls, tugging so hard that I jerk in place.

"Did you tell him that I forced you? Huh?" Something in his voice tugs at my consciousness through the building heat. An emotion. What is it? "Or maybe you came clean to him? Perhaps *he's* the one encouraging you? I wouldn't put it past him. The old man thinks a woman might save me—" A hiss rips from my lips as he tightens his grip on my hair, forcing my attention back to him. "Is that it?"

I risk more pain to shake my head. "N-no—"

"Maybe you're right." There it is again. That subtle dip in his inflection. Guilt? Fear? Suddenly, the answer comes to me. *Shame.* He cares about what Vanya thinks of him. "Vanya isn't that selfish. He'd think you're too good for me. Too innocent. Damn, you have him fooled."

His thumb continues its deliberate descent, grazing me beneath the denim. I'm still sore from the night before. I haven't washed. Wet, tender skin is an easy target. When he shoves his hand down the front of my pants, my body turns against me; muscles and nerves take on a life of their own. My thighs jerk. Spread.

"Maybe this is all your doing? Your plan to stay alive?" Mischa demands. His fingers cup me fully even though his seed is still there, drying between my legs. Rather than cringe in disgust, his hand twitches at the realization, stroking… "Are you really that desperate?"

"Y-yes." The word comes unbidden as his fingers still. My hips jerk, seeking out his touch. I need it. Dark thoughts in my head battle for supremacy. But this…

As humiliating, and wrong, and terrible as it is. *This* keeps it all at bay like nothing else.

But I've angered him again. His thumb flicks against my needy flesh, nowhere near hard enough. Punishing me.

"Robert must like his whores cock-hungry," he hisses into my ear while his thumb laves a slow, cruel circle along my entrance.

Cock-hungry. My inner muscles clench at the word. The raspy, dangerous way that he says it. Cock. His cock. Inside me.

My eyes flutter shut at the thought. The air feels thicker. My teeth descend into my bottom lip without permission, maintaining what little pride I have left by locking away a moan.

"What the fuck are you?" Mischa asks, flexing his fingers, dipping them inside me. "Do you really think this changes anything?"

Of course I don't. Not even as my hands grip the seat on either side of me, my nails breaking off against the leather. That pressure begins to build again, sweltering in my stomach. Spreading. Tightening.

And then, just when I fear it might boil over...

He pulls his hand away.

Before I can regain my senses, something nudges my lower lip, ripe with the musky scent of me. It's like I know what he wants before he even grates out the vulgar request through clenched teeth.

"Suck it."

My tongue shoots out, tentatively brushing the rough pad of a finger. I taste myself. His sweat.

I swallow it down.

"Fuck." He shoves away from me.

I open my eyes and find him glaring toward the front of the van. My legs are still spread, my pants hanging open. Slowly, I draw my knees together, hissing at the pressure still mounting between them. My fingers shake as they redo my zipper, but the tight confines of the denim aggravate the reckless heat he already started.

Cock-hungry. Cock-hungry. That phrase circles the inside of my skull incessantly. I can't escape it. I can't escape *him*.

My only refuge is found when I close my eyes and focus on my shallow breathing. Only now do I dip into the one arsenal I have against Mischa. I think of Robert. His face. His mocking, lethal smile. His brown, soulless eyes.

I remember the words he told me nightly, smothered against my hair.

"You belong to me, Elle. You belong to me..."

CHAPTER 14

"Get up."

A car door slams in addition to the shout, snapping me awake. We're here. Wherever here is. A hotel? As I peel my eyes open, I make out a shape looming in the darkness. Tall. Grand. A house? It's nearly twice the size of Winthorp Manor, casting an impressive silhouette, even in the dark.

"I said get up," someone commands. Mischa.

I scramble in the direction of his voice, stepping out onto a paved courtyard. A grand array of stone steps lead to the front of the house. The lair of another criminal who deals in cocaine?

No… Mischa's posture is too relaxed for that, and his past words to Vanya spring to mind. *We're going home.*

There's an undeniable familiarity as he mounts the steps with me in his wake. Around us, the other vans park and the men disperse, carrying various materials in different directions on the property. I expect Mischa to shove me aside or direct me to Vanya.

But no.

I'm the sole possession he hauls with him to the front door of the mansion while his men clutch their guns and fall in beside us. I'm his *captive*, dragged across a grand entrance and up a winding staircase too quickly to even get my bearings or take in the finery.

His shoulders serve as my only scenery. Tense, solid muscle.

I'm not sure which direction he takes me in. I only know when he stops—at the mouth of a room with solid oak floors and a bed in the center.

It's his. I smell him on the air, faint, as if he hasn't been here in a while. The black sheets still contain some part of him, however. It's a far cry from the lumpy mattresses he's dominated before now.

"Take off your clothes." He issues the command while slamming the door behind us, twisting the lock.

It's a test. For some reason, he feels the need to try me in this arena. Like Robert, he's addicted to this violent game.

But Robert never broke the rules. Impatient, Mischa rushes me from behind and strips me himself.

There's no finesse in the way he yanks my jeans down my legs for the second time. There's no predatory care taken to heighten my fear with every touch. His erection pulses against the base of my spine. Thick. Heavy. Like a steel rod encased in denim.

"Get on the fucking bed." He shoves me forward.

I obey the command, mounting the mattress on my hands and knees. For a split second, I'm back with Robert, trapped inside his private suite while he runs his hand down my spine and watches me tremble.

"Beg," he'd prompt me, like always.

"Jesus Christ, you're perfect," Mischa growls, fury lacing every word. *"Too* perfect." He shoves his palm against my ass, making enough room for him to brace himself behind me. His fingers return between my legs, finding that same slickness from before. "Fucking hell." A sound rumbles from him I've never heard a human make. Deep. Throaty.

It rips through me, leaving me quaking in the aftermath.

"You…you're wet for me, Little One," he accuses in a tone that proclaims it's the worst possible offense I could have committed against him. "Say it."

My lips move of their own accord, breathing the words against the silken comforter in front of me. "I'm wet for you."

"Damn." He doesn't expect the candor, sucking in a breath. A grunt breaks loose when he exhales, his breath fanning the back of my neck. "Say it again."

My entire body shivers beneath the weight of such an insane command. I obey anyway. "I…I'm wet for you."

Hissing, he rears back, forcing his legs between mine so that I'm straddling him from behind. He hooks his knees against me and spreads his open, forcing mine to part even wider. I have to brace my hands against the mattress for balance while he slides his fingers beneath me, cupping my thigh.

"Then show me." His erection nuzzles that tender place between my thighs, impossibly hard.

Without thinking, I reach for it, blindly wrapping my hand around the base.

"Easy," he snaps, grasping my wrist and forcing my grip to loosen. "Slower," he explains. "Like this."

Numb to reality, I keep going. He hums low in his throat as I stroke him from end to tip and my mind reels. He feels terrifyingly big. How the hell did he ever fit inside me?

My grip falters as he grows slicker with sweat. I have to rely on him more to support my weight. My knees shake, threatening to pitch me over at any second. I'm too far gone to give a damn about anything but this. His teeth graze my throat without a shred of gentleness or mercy. Just naked, scorching lust. The slower my hand moves, the more his cock twitches impatiently, until finally he bucks out of my grip altogether.

"I see it now," he tells me. "Why he wants you back so fucking badly."

I whimper as his teeth seize a chunk of skin, grinding it between them. My eyelids flutter, my spine curling and driving my hips against him. Nothing describes how it feels when his crown grazes my entrance. Nothing.

I'm still gasping at the feeling when his hand finds mine, guiding me to the sliver of space between us. He forces my fingers to curl and places them along the ridge of his shaft. Then he arches his hips, wedging the tip of himself between my folds. "Put me inside you."

My eyes widen. Robert would never issue such an insane request. He'd never give me that kind of control. Over him. Over myself.

But it's not surrender Mischa offers as he allows me to steer him inside me inch by painful inch. It's possession in an entirely different way than domination. It's madness.

It's fucking unbearable.

I can't stifle my moan. It trickles out of me, high and tight as my head falls back against his shoulder. Once again, he sinks in easily. Too deep. Too real. Desperate, my nails scrape at his hips, hunting for stability. Just when I find a position that works, he lunges, shoving me onto my hands and knees.

The mattress trembles as he rears back and slips from my grasping channel. Before I can even catch my breath, he slides back in.

And then he fucks me.

I forget everything but how to breathe. I forget my own fucking name. The fact that he has no soul. His cruelty.

Each drive of his hips pushes a tiny bit of *my* soul out. Through my pores. My throat.

Robert made a boast once. *I'll fuck your brains out.*

He never came close.

Mischa drives my entire being out of my body, forcing himself into the empty spaces left behind. He's primal, inching our bodies closer to the headboard with every thrust. Closer. Close. My fingers are braced against the wood before I know it, and his hands tighten over my hips, pulling me into him with every brutal claiming.

I'm painfully aware of the fact that *he* is the one inside me. The one demolishing me. No one else. For once, my thoughts only contain a single name and it spills from my lips like a prayer. "Mischa—"

Blood rushes to my head as his fingers find my neck and squeeze. He shoves me down, pinning my face to the mattress. "Again," he grates out between pants. "Say…again."

I do and the final thrust undoes him. He comes with an intensity that catches me off guard. Molten energy spills into me without a valve to slow the overwhelming pace. The last spurt has barely entered me before he draws back, letting me collapse breathless against the twisted sheets.

I hear the hiss of a zipper being redone. Then footsteps retreat from the room. A door opens.

Slams.

And I'm alone.

I don't wait for shame to descend this time. In the aftermath of the chaos, I manage to scrape together what's left of my pride and gingerly stagger to my feet. The room is not only spacious, but grander than I first realized. The furniture is old but well maintained: polished oak. Just where are we?

The light fixtures are silver, made of delicate designs that resemble vines twisting from the paneled walls. It's a style that reminds me of Winthorp Manor's—at least before Briar convinced her father to "update" some of the interior rooms.

The smell here is the same. Old. Prestigious. Unwelcoming.

For all its grandeur, this room could be no less personal than the one in the hotel, but subtle clues lurk in plain sight. The black sheets are of the highest quality. A polished dresser contains a neat array of men's clothing. Not gray fatigues, but shirts and slacks. There's an en suite bathroom grander than the one attached to my room in Robert's suite. The floors are gleaming obsidian marble. There're a sunken tub and a separate enclosed shower. Granite countertops support a double sink, while the polished mirror above them displays a reflection that appears hideously out of place among the finery.

The shadow of Robert's wife stares back at me with hollow eyes. She seems so lost. So broken. Her healing wounds look even worse in the soft glow cast by the ornate light fixtures that illuminate the room.

Mischa's brand screams against my pale skin. My right eye is purple, partially shut beneath swelling. My neck is reddened, my body a collage of scars and bruises both new and old. It should be hard to discern what marks were left by Robert and those inflicted by Mischa. Hard, but not impossible. Robert is methodical in his madness. He placed his wounds strategically, with thought and care put into every scrape, scratch, and cut.

Mischa is reckless. My body isn't his canvas. It's his plaything.

Which is worse? To be used slowly and sparingly? Or to be chewed and swallowed alive?

My eyes water in my reflection and I turn away, unwilling to learn the answer.

Were I to play by Robert's rules, my next action would be to huddle on the middle of the bed and wait for his return. Only then could I bathe, and change the sheets, and finally rebuild my armor piece by piece. He'd break me down all over again, but that was the point. He liked me cleanly refreshed like a reset game board.

Now...

I run the bath, turning the water to scalding. Lying in the center of the tub, I wait until the water reaches my chin, bathing sore, battered limbs. I let time wash the pain away while my heartbeat settles into a gentle rhythm. In this sliver of peace, I try to forget both the man I was taken from and the man still inside me.

One dies quietly, his memories easily silenced.

The other…lingers. I smell him, even here. His flavor develops on the tip of my tongue, making it impossible to forget that I don't crave him how a woman should want a man. I don't want softness. No, I'm addicted to the sting of his poison. I like the way it feels when it's dribbled into my open wounds. The pain is different from what I'm used to. A distraction.

A drug.

My heartbeat flutters even before I sense that I'm no longer alone. I feel his breath first, ruffling my damp hair and basting my wet flesh. Alarmed, I fling my eyes open to his hardened expression. His narrow as they take in my half-submerged body. Is he surprised by my deviation from our usual script?

If so, he hides his shock well. The muscles in his arms ripple as he crosses them over his chest and cocks his head in an animalistic manner, like a wolf sizing up half-eaten prey. Does it deserve a killing blow yet? Or should it suffer a little longer?

"I want to know who you are," he says without revealing his final decision. "Not that bullshit you spewed before. Who you are *really*."

What a question. I draw my knees beneath my chin, wrapping my arms around them. Hot water continues to flood in, causing steam to waft from the surface. "I…I don't know what you mean—"

"Start with your parents," he suggests gruffly, "Who were they?"

"I never knew my father," I admit. "And my mother was a maid—"

"Don't." Suddenly, he's crouched beside the tub. The shadow he casts over the water reinforces his presence without him even having to touch me. "Don't lie to me, Little One," he warns. "You think I haven't shown my mercy when you have before? You thought I didn't notice?"

A shudder runs down my spine, making the water slosh against the sides of the tub. It's not fear of him that triggers the reaction, but of the words he wants to hear. The ones I've locked away for over twenty-three years.

Slowly, I draw in a ragged breath and brace the whole side of my face against my knee, eyeing the wall opposite him.

"My mother's name was Marnie Winthorp," I say haltingly. There's no point in holding anything back, so I don't. "*Yes,* that Marnie. *Yes,* Robert Sr.'s second wife. *Yes,* Briar's mother."

Our mother.

"But," I add haltingly. "I am not Robert Sr.'s daughter."

CHAPTER 15

"Marnie was your mother. How?"

I stiffen at how he voices that question. Cautious, not shocked. Intrigued, not disbelieving. It's almost as if he knew—or at least suspected the truth all along. Which is impossible. Unless Robert slipped in the handling of his most closely guarded secret.

The burning desire to know for sure gives me the strength to glance over my shoulder to decipher Mischa's expression for myself. He can't even hide the curiosity glinting in his eyes.

"I'm not sure," I admit. "All anyone ever told me was that she left the manor shortly after Briar was born—"

"Left?" He stresses the word, coating it in a warning.

"Yes," I say. "I don't know why. A year later, she returned, pregnant with me. Robert, out of mercy, let her keep me, as long as she didn't claim I was his and kept her indiscretion quiet."

Though, ironically, he was the one who never let anyone forget it.

"And you know nothing about your father?" Mischa prods.

"No. She never mentioned who he was."

"And you're sure of that?"

Again, he sounds too careful. As if he knows a secret puzzle piece missing from the narrative that I've yet to see for myself. Something to explain the sadness that coated my mother's features like paint, perhaps? It's a dark thought I can't escape. In a futile attempt to, I risk facing him directly—and instantly regret the action.

He's cold again, eyeing me as if I'm something best viewed from a distance. A threat. An enemy to be conquered.

My body burns, remembering what it meant to be at his mercy, and I wrap my arms tighter around my knees—not that I can escape his scrutiny for very long.

"So you lived there, in that fucking manor."

I nod, almost grateful for the change in subject. "Yes. I grew up alongside Briar, but she was more my mistress than my sister. I played with her. I cleaned up after her. I..." *Loved her.* "I didn't know about the plan," I say instead. "That I was a decoy. I didn't... She asked me to join her at her wedding," I admit, not recognizing the hard note in my own voice. The memories of that day hurt twice as much to relive with him watching. How happy I was. How naïve. How foolish. "She bought me new clothes. She did my hair... I didn't know."

If he believes me, he says nothing and lets the silence linger between us while my own thoughts fester and feed on what little sanity I have left.

Finally, he asks, "And your husband?"

"Robert?" I inhale and exhale slowly, steeling myself for the next phase in my sordid tale. "He wasn't cruel to me, growing up," I admit. "His mother died when he was young and he rarely spent time at the manor. Though, when he did come home from school, he was never malicious. Some could say he protected me."

Or saved me for himself.

"When I turned nineteen, he expressed his interest. I accepted it, knowing full well what that would mean."

I suppose I learned that lesson as a child: he taught me who the real monster was all along.

"He never raped me." It feels important to say that. With rape, there was a victim. My body, however, had been sacrificed.

But did that make it any easier to bear?

My heart shies from the answer. *No.*

"I knew that he had f-fetishes," I add thickly. "I knew he could be violent. I knew that being with him would be an ordeal within itself. But he was better than—" A sudden tightness in my throat chokes off my voice. My wounded cheek burns as tiny ripples form in the water around my chin, created by falling tears. "I made my choice," I force myself to say. Hearing it out loud stings like nothing else. Not a million jagged cuts or bruises.

But Mischa isn't swayed by my emotions. He phrases an even crueler question as my tears continue to fall. "And me? You really think you remember me?"

"I remember a boy," I counter. "Someone who looked at me and showed me..."

What? An ounce of humanity?

"M-mercy," I decide, sucking in a breath. "He showed me mercy—"

"Don't pretend!"

I jump as his fingers slam against the rim of the tub, curling around the polished edge.

"You think I don't fucking know what game you're playing? That I can't smell it on you?" His nostrils flare as if to steal my scent. "*Cunning*. You feign your innocent act pretty well, but I've had more skilled women try to seduce me. Do you really think sex and false memories will make me pity you?" When I don't speak, he grabs my chin, grinding his fingers into my jawline. "Fucking say it. Admit why you let me..."

Fuck you.

Is there a reason? One springs to my lips of its own accord. "I-I deserve it." I don't know where the words came from. Why they hurt so much to say. Why a part of me feels like they were ripped from some vital part of my soul even Robert couldn't reach.

If being around him has taught me one thing, it's that all sinners receive their punishment eventually.

"Deserve?" Surprise flickers across Mischa's gaze for a split second before he lets me go and rises to his feet. "Trust a Winthorp to use sex as a punishment," he mutters, laughing coldly at the irony. Without warning, he whirls on his heel and slams his fist against the wall with a thud that resonates through my entire being.

Tense with anticipation, I wait for him to leave. To storm off.

Instead…

"Turn off the water."

My pulse surges as I lunge for the faucet and switch it off.

"We're not done," he says, turning the full brunt of his gaze on me once again. My mind plays a dangerous game of roulette as I try to guess where his next question might lead. "You said your husband made you keep numbers for him…"

"Y-yes."

"And you remember them? Don't waste your breath lying to me again."

I just nod, too exhausted to keep up the charade. Robert's secrets are my last to tell. "Every amount," I admit with a heavy sigh. "Every name."

It was the final act of our game in a poetic sense. Robert gave me enough to destroy him. Then he locked me up tight and dared me to leave him. Was it his father's idea to use me in his safety net for Briar? Had he let his son in on such a plan?

I'm not sure. The Winthorps have their own inner language of tricks and power grabs played between them, with a convoluted tally no outsider could fathom.

"You want me to give his accounts to you." It's not a question, and he doesn't bother denying it. "And if I do…will you still sell me?"

There's no playing coy with him. He frowns at my attempt, his eyes flashing midnight. "And why shouldn't I? I've experienced what you have to offer," he reminds me, making my cheeks flame. "Forget the five thousand Boris offered. I could easily charge double."

Somehow, I manage to ignore the ferocity of the threat—no, his promise. I run my tongue over my cracked lips, tasting dried blood. "Do you really think you can beat the numbers out of me?"

It's not a taunt as much as it is a genuine question. Can this man best Robert Winthorp at a game of his creation? Does he really have what it takes to rip the truth from my head?

Of course he does.

But does he have the time?

Precious minutes pass at his discretion, but the truth is clear: He doesn't.

"I'll give you all I know," I propose. "All I ask is that you don't sell me as a whore. I won't try to run. I won't resist. I won't fight when you…"

When you kill me.

"I swear," I continue. "All I ask is that you do with me what you want. I don't care. But don't barter my body."

It's a pathetic, simple request. Or so I believe, until I make the mistake of looking into his eyes and witness the darkness brewing there. The open hatred, so raw and consuming that it steals my breath away.

"You think that you can make demands of me?" His voice breaks into two bone-chilling notes. One low and hollow, the other guttural. Animalistic.

"N-no," I stammer before he can finish taking a step in my direction. "I only want…your mercy."

It's a word that I suspect would mean nothing to another man. A better man.

For him? It's a trigger. *Boom!* I've blown the lid off his rage without even trying.

"Mercy?" He's on his knees before I can blink, reaching into the tub for my throat, clenching the already sore flesh. "You think that you can demand *mercy* from me? Do you even know what that word fucking means?"

"N-not demand," I clarify, wheezing in my effort to get the words past his tightening grip. "Asking…for it."

Begging.

He tilts my head back while simultaneously leaning closer, heedless of the tremor that quakes through me in response. With that cold, piercing gaze as his weapon, he slices me open and searches beneath my skin, hunting down any hint of deceit. Finally, he draws back.

"I don't barter with *dead* women," he spits. "Or whores. Or the wives of my fucking enemies—"

"What about a human being?" I wonder softly, marveling at the fact that I've challenged him at all.

His fingers tighten in a silent threat, but I can still breathe. For now.

"Someone who has nothing left to lose?"

He chuckles at that and cocks his head to view me from a different angle. "And let's say I don't sell you. Am I supposed to care for two fucking 'human beings' out of the kindness of my soul, Little One? At least until I slit your throat?"

Two?

He laughs again as my brow furrows. "How quickly you fucking forget," he scolds. "The girl you protected. Nicolai's. I can't let her go. She already knows too much."

No. My veins run cold with ice. "You wouldn't…"

"I will. I can't keep her here out of charity. So, if I don't sell *you*, are you willing to have her be put in your place?"

No. I shake my head, feeling the ridge of his knuckles with every frantic movement. When he lets me go, I stare down at the water and fight to keep the fire building behind my eyes at bay. There's no use in admitting my defeat out loud.

Regardless, rare anger bubbles beneath my skin. Only the most subhuman of men use child pawns in their wicked games.

"There's something you want to say, Little One." Mischa runs his thumb along the bruised side of my face in a terrifying display of encouragement. "Go on. Say it."

My lips unlock painfully. "For someone who claims to hate Robert Sr. so much…you seem determined to emulate him."

I expect a blow as punishment. My shoulders tense in a futile effort to brace for its impact. Instead, Mischa laughs again. He growls. Aware of his shadow flickering over the floor, I infer that he moves to a corner of the bathroom and snatches something from the wall, which he then throws at me. It bounces off my head and lands partially in the water. A white towel.

"Get out," he tells me, his voice strained with that dangerous calm I've come to fear.

After releasing the stopper to allow the water to drain, I climb from the tub, draping the towel around my shoulders. Left with no choice, I follow Mischa into the main bedroom. Without a glance spared in my direction, he enters the hallway. Still wet, with only the towel to cover myself with, I'm forced to weigh embarrassment with obedience.

With Robert, my choice would have been clear.

Now? I turn my gaze to the wooden dresser and wrench a drawer open without giving myself the time to weigh the consequences. The first shirt my fingers fall over is black, finely tailored. Letting the towel drop to my feet, I scramble into the dress shirt, surprised to find that it reaches past my knees.

As my damp hair falls over my shoulders, I creep to the doorway and find Mischa waiting paces away. His eyes sweep over me once and then narrow.

"I suggest you remember those accounts, Little One," he warns before turning on his heel and marching down the corridor. "Come. It's time to prove just how valuable you are to your husband."

CHAPTER 16

We don't go far. A few closed doors down, he stops before another doorway and passes through it. There's a desk in the center of this room, with two leather chairs placed before it. A study? It's simpler in appearance, but it reminds me of the grand one where Robert Sr. holds court—a place I'm only ever allowed to venture in his son's presence.

In silence, Mischa approaches the solid oak desk and grabs something from its surface. A leather-bound book. He offers it to me, along with a silver pen. "Let's see how well your husband trained you, Little One," he taunts.

Slowly, I lower myself onto one of the chairs and I open the book to a blank page. Balancing it over my lap, I uncap the pen and place the nib down over the ivory parchment. Four names and four amounts—that's what I give him, fished at random from the recesses of my mind. It's nowhere near everything.

And he knows it. Still, he accepts the book when I hold it out to him and scans what I've written.

"This name," he says, pointing to the third entry down. "What do you know about it?"

"Barklow," I read aloud. I look down at my lap, turning my focus inward. "Tall man. Blond. Balding. He met with Robert at least once every few months." About what? I don't know.

Something tells me Mischa has a suspicion though. He nods to himself as if tucking that bit of knowledge away for later. "And what else?"

I stare at the floor, averting my gaze from his. "I…I can't remember."

"Oh?" He takes a step toward me, reaching out to run his fingers through my wet hair. Roughly. I flinch as they snag on a knotted tangle. "I wonder if I can refresh your memory?"

"You don't have to threaten me," I say, looking up to meet his gaze directly. "Even by giving you only four names, you know what that means…"

I've betrayed my husband. It's a reality that hasn't sunken in yet. I don't feel the fear I should. At least not yet.

"I'm tired," I insist, allowing my exhaustion to leak into my voice. "I haven't eaten in…" Hell, only he knows the exact answer to that. "There's no point in only committing half treason," I add weakly.

"And who says you'll last another day?" Mischa wonders. He lets the statement linger on the air between us, an unmistakable reminder of where we stand.

My life is extended only at his whim.

Not that I could ever forget.

"Starving me may be an enterprising way to conserve resources if you plan on killing me soon," I admit. "But it won't make me remember any faster."

"And how do I know if you have anything *worth* remembering?" he counters.

I lift my shoulder in a weak attempt at a shrug. "You wouldn't be asking if you knew that I didn't."

It's a dangerous game to mince words with him. I half-expect his anger to take hold once again. Instead, he surprises me by returning his attention to the book.

"You know more of your husband's accounts?" he muses openly.

Aware of him watching, I fold my hands together and rest them on my lap. Lying would be useless, so I say nothing. Finally, his fingers seize a chunk of my hair and he uses it as a leash to force me to meet his gaze directly.

"So, you are hungry, Little One?" he asks in a lethal murmur.

My stomach answers for me, grumbling loudly. Amused, Mischa tilts his head to the side, allowing his tongue to shoot out along his lower lip. Fire spreads through my stomach as my heart thumps unsteadily at the motion.

"Then ask me for food."

I don't hesitate. "Please."

"And you want to sleep?" He phrases the question in a way that reminds me of a hunter priming a trap.

"Y-yes."

"And you think that what you can offer me is *worth* those resources, Little One? The mere promise that you might have more to give? Your trust is truly worth that much?"

Is it? I honestly don't know. "Robert doesn't gamble," I tell him. "So...I don't know much about favorable odds."

"No?" The corner of his mouth quirks, but even that brief bit of emotion can't touch the coldness in his eyes. "You do seem to know a thing or two about Roulette, Little One," he suspects. "So we will play."

He turns to the doorway, beckoning me to follow with a nod of his chin. This time, he leads me back to the ornate entrance and I'm allowed to take more details of the interior in than before.

A crystal chandelier bathes the grand hall in a warm, orange glow, illuminating curved archways leading off into various corridors. When Mischa turns down one, I follow, keeping as much distance between us as I dare to.

"Here." He comes to a stop near an open doorway. Beyond it is a dining room with a long oak table and windows framed in cream curtains. "Sit," he commands.

I slip past him and take the seat farthest from his position. He laughs at the display, and I presume that he writes it off as an act of fear. But no. I can see him more clearly from here. How he stands. The tension in his posture. The way he hones his gaze on me as if it's the only way he can keep from looking at anything else. Then he leaves, and I know instinctively not to move.

I sit. I wait. His games aren't as predictable as Robert's. He leaves me guessing by the end of each round. He lets me sweat. Where my husband sought only to amuse himself with my pain, Mischa seeks to...

Ruin me. In any way he can. With brutality. With violent sex. With stingy mercy?

I tense as he reappears at the mouth of the room, holding a plate in his hand. The food on it is simple: a sandwich and scattered potato chips. My stomach pangs for it anyway, and I fight to keep utterly still as he carries the plate to me. When he stops beside my chair, I expect another display of dominance. *Beg. Ask.*

Instead, he unceremoniously slams the offering down, and I don't wait for his permission. I grab the sandwich, rip it in half, and shove as much as I can into my mouth at one time. In three gulping bites, I choke it down and start on the chips like a damn animal.

Ellen Winthorp dined with decorum. She ate her food from her husband's hand or devoured it slowly with whatever knife or fork the occasion called for.

That woman is dead. In Mischa's realm, there are no manners. Jus*t taking*—whatever I can before he rips it out of reach.

"And sleep," he says once I've cleared the plate, continuing our conversation as if never interrupted. "You wanted that as well…"

"Yes," I cautiously reply.

"Then come."

Grappling with a partially filled stomach, I trail him back up the stairs and into his room. The bed isn't meant for me. I know that even before he reaches down to tug his boots off and approach the mattress himself. "So sleep," he mockingly goads.

My eyes fall over the corner beside the dresser. I approach it, prepared to sink down and rest my head against the wall.

"No." He snaps his fingers, forcing my attention on him. He's seated, lying back against the headboard, his legs extended before him. "My floor is too good for you, Little One." He waves his hand, commanding me closer. It's only as he spreads his legs just enough to reveal a sliver of space between them that I realize just what he intends. "I said you could sleep, but I never said peacefully, did I? I will be waiting for you in your dreams." The malice in his voice robs my lungs of air. "You will smell me. Feel me. Taste me. I won't let you escape, even for a second." He nods toward his chest. "Now, sleep."

I strip my face of emotion as I lower myself beside him onto the bed. Then I turn and brace a trembling hand against his shoulder, finding enough leverage to sink against him, trapped on either side by a massive thigh. His breath scalds the top of my head while his heartbeat thunders beneath me. He's right. I taste him. His scent floods my nostrils. A cold, sickening certainty fills me as I let my eyes drift shut with the bruised side of my face against his chest.

I'll dream of him.

I'll die of him.

CHAPTER 17

*P*risoners have no right to make demands. So I pray instead to whatever higher power will listen. For ruthless, vile destruction. *Amen.*

Torment is what I crave—at least when it comes to Mischa. Torment I can barely handle. Torture my body can only just withstand.

Pain, pain, pain.

It's the only way I can compare him to Robert, measuring their varying flavors of agony inflicted.

But there is no comparison to *this*. There is no chilling memory in my head to examine this scenario through. On the rare shred of untouched space on my psyche, Mischa carves a new terrifying ordeal to relive.

As promised, I dream of him.

And I wake up knowing what true hell is. It's not the measured cruelty Robert dished out. It's not fearful memories or repulsive scars. It's peace—being able to find it, even for a second, while in the arms of a monster.

What a terrible power to lord over someone.

The moment I regain my senses, my eyes fly open and I view the room from behind a cage composed of muscular, tattooed limbs. Regaining my bearings feels like assembling the pieces of a crudely made puzzle. It's morning. Gray daylight glimmers around the edges of the curtains. Beneath my ear, a steady heartbeat taps out a constant rhythm while thick fingers twist through my hair…

Not tugging for once. Just feeling, rubbing the strands together and testing their weight.

"You don't like to be held," Mischa declares as my body stiffens while his fingers brush my scalp. "You tremble in your sleep. You flinch."

He didn't sleep himself; I can hear it in his coarse tone. No, he studied. How to strip me bare and catch me off guard.

As if aware of my suspicions, he flattens his hand against my skull, applying slight pressure. "Your husband was lenient with you," he adds knowingly. "He kept you skittish."

Is that what he calls it?

"You know how they test when soldiers are ready for war? When they're broken enough?" He untangles one of his hands from my hair and snatches my wrist, displaying each finger. "They're ordered to stick their hands in an open flame, but it's not enough to just obey. Only a few can stand to watch their skin peel and burn until they're given the order to pull their hand away. *They are ready*. But those who flinch out of reach before the command is given…" He manually places my hand on his hip, watching how it quivers. "They are pathetic fools. Poorly trained."

Like young boys who leave little girls untouched?

I'm not brave enough to ask. When he releases me, I make the mistake of believing that he's made his point, ended the game. My heart races as I plan my escape. Cautiously, I brace one of my hands over the mattress and attempt to push myself upright.

One fierce tug on my scalp shoves me right back down. "Did I say you could move?"

But I need to. I can only ignore his nearness for so long. His thighs create a stifling prison, trapping me within a cage I'm not used to. He's right: Robert never wielded physical touch as a weapon. He slept beside me sparingly, only as his idea of a treat after a particularly brutal session. He never held me in his arms simply to prove a point.

But that highlights another difference between my husband and my captor: Robert wanted me somewhat whole.

Mischa wants me utterly broken, in pieces too small to ever resemble their original shape.

He extends his torture long enough to ensure I learn the rules. Only *he* can dictate how much I move my head and how much of him I feel against my aching, battered frame. But he can't control one aspect of his anatomy…

It slams against my stomach with every breath I take, dangerously hard. I cringe away from the contact as much as I can, and he chuckles, twisting his fingers more harshly through my hair.

"Don't act shy now." It's not a taunt, but a dare. "I'm sure your husband didn't let you rest for long—"

"I...I'm not on birth control." I don't know why I chose to admit that to him. Considering his threats to end my life, it doesn't really matter. Maybe I subconsciously needed to voice another comparison between him and Robert out loud.

While Robert hated the medicine behind hormone-manipulating drugs, he studied my cycle religiously, planning his "needs" around the days that would be most beneficial to him.

As expected, Mischa laughs, shrugging his shoulder. "Pregnancy is your last concern, Little One," he says, letting a lethal implication lurk in between the words. "But..." As he forms a fist and nudges my hip with the tops of his knuckles, I stiffen. "You've had a child before. I saw the scar."

Scar. Warily, my fingers creep to the mark in question, tracing it through the fabric of his shirt. It's one of the few I never observed in much detail. I can only recall its general shape: a curved, jagged line at the base of my abdomen. After a few brief seconds, I let my hand fall.

"Did your husband keep that a secret as well?" He nudges me more firmly when I don't answer.

But fear can't override every instinct, as it turns out. My teeth clamp down over an answer. My brain won't betray those memories. I'm forced to endure his curiosity for nearly a minute before he shifts his weight and knocks me off him without pressing the topic further.

"Get up."

I scramble onto my hands and knees and back away to the opposite end of the mattress. He watches me go with an unreadable expression before he stands and strips his shirt, tossing it onto the floor.

My brain short-circuits as I take him in. A collage of scars and varying tattoos mark his body like it's a vandalized canvas. Long, vicious marks. Snarling black skulls and swirling designs with undiscernible meanings. I'm not sure why my gaze settles over one brand in particular, sliced into his lower back. It's large enough to span nearly his entire torso, neatly integrated through several surrounding tattoos. A complex series of scars forms its construction: two vertical slashes beside a crudely etched V. Another Roman numeral? *Seven.*

The longer I stare, the more unsteady the world feels beneath me. With Robert, curiosity was a warning sign to back away from whatever sparked it. Nothing good ever came from learning his secrets.

With Mischa…

That same emotion is a drug, numbing me to the harsher reality. The promise of his secrets doesn't repulse me as much as it confuses me. Maybe because I can't escape the pathetic truth: I want to learn…everything.

I want to know what made him human once. Robert wasn't a monster so much as he was a beast. He was born that way. He'll die that way.

He doesn't use his body as a canvas to illustrate his descent into madness.

He has no Vanya mourning what he used to be.

Does the difference mean a damn thing?

Maybe…

"See something you like?" Mischa wonders, his cold tone snapping me back to reality.

I turn my focus to the wall beyond his head as he continues toward the dresser, swiping a clean shirt from one of the drawers. I hear a zipper come undone moments later, but when he finally reenters my line of sight, he's fully dressed in a pair of slacks and a lazily donned button-down. He fastened it up to his chest, leaving a sliver of defaced skin in view.

"Let's hope that sleep refreshed your memory," he warns before exiting the room altogether, leaving me to follow on shaking legs.

Morning casts an alarming pallor over the grand estate, and the daylight seeping in reveals secrets skillfully hidden by the dark. His men are a constant presence, lurking around doorways and wandering the ornate halls. There's a staleness to the wealth, like something long since abandoned.

Why?

The wooden floors and paneled walls reveal no answers by the time I'm led inside the barren office, forced to take a seat before the desk. Mischa hands me the leather book, which was still where he'd left it. I dutifully flip it open to a clean page and balance the pen between my fingers.

Memory is a dangerously unreliable thing. It's there, fighting to be known when you're desperate to suppress it. Yet it hides when you need it, obscuring details and blurring lines. Mischa watches, patiently impatient as I etch out another four names in painstaking fashion.

Upon snatching the book from me, he scans the page, his eyes narrowing over the entries. Then he rips it from the book and shoves it crumpled into his pocket. "More." He drops the book onto my lap and jerks his chin toward the pen. "Write them."

"I can't." My hand trembles, allowing the nib of the pen to broadcast my anxiety on the air. "It…it doesn't work like that—"

"Like what?" he presses, lethally soft. His hand cups my chin, wrenching it back so that my gaze meets his. "What doesn't work?"

I swallow hard, consumed by the vast emptiness that paints his irises. I always thought Robert was hard to interpret, but now, I know the truth. Robert hid nothing behind his darkness. There were no secrets to discern.

"I can't just turn it off and on," I admit. "M-maybe…if you told me what you were looking for—"

"Ha!" He lets me go and throws his head back for another chilling laugh. "Don't, Little One," he warns. "Don't attempt to manipulate me. I am not Ivan."

I don't know what he means. Looking down at my hands, I try again. "There are hundreds of names. Thousands of accounts—"

"Then give me the ones that you heard the most." His tone is less mocking this time. Something odd taints his expression and I struggle to name it. Actual interest? "Think." He comes up behind me to hiss the word directly into my ear. "Think hard, Little One. I suggest you hold my attention for as long as you have it."

My body resonates with the ominous suggestion, and I return the pen to the page. Three names spring to mind and I scribble them hastily, one after the other. When I hold them out to Mischa, I expect him to shove the book back in my face with a growled command. *More!*

But his eyes spark with interest as he fingers one name in particular. "Son of a bitch…" His gaze flicks up, burning through mine. "Him. How do you know him?"

I scan the letters partially obscured by his pointing thumb. *Kostas.* My stomach tightens ominously. *That* name. It's one of the few I can trace back to a clear memory. Several memories. He was one of the few men Robert made me pleasure for him. With my mouth. My hands. They tremble as the coarse images linger on my conscience.

Mischa says something else, snapping his fingers when I don't answer. Or at least it appears he does. I hear nothing. Just deep, masculine groans smothered on the air, paired with the burning humiliation of being used.

"Hey—"

I violently cringe from the hand that brushes my cheek. Beneath me, the chair slides against the wood, driven by the sudden shift in my weight. My eyes blink rapidly, but I'm not in Robert's room. And the man before me, he's…

Terrifying. I've never seen that kind of rage reflected on the face of a human being. It's raw. Animalistic.

It's…not directed at *me.*

"No," he snarls, gritting the word between his teeth. Deliberately, his hand comes for me again, cupping the side of my throat. "You don't flinch from me." Each finger tenses against my windpipe, but not to choke for once. To feel. To reinforce his presence. *You don't flinch.*

And I don't. Robert relished making me squirm. He chuckled whenever I jumped at the mercy of his fingertips. But I'd give anything to emulate that reaction now. Anything.

When Mischa captures my chin in his palm, I don't recoil. I shiver. It's a subtle difference that I feel down to the very nerves running beneath my skin. Fear is one thing. Anticipation is something different entirely. It's harder to stomach. Harder to reconcile with the rules I've lived by for so long.

"Tell me," he commands, urging me to face him. "What… Did he hurt you?"

He didn't mean to phrase the question so heatedly. His eyes narrow, directing that anger inward for a rare split second.

But he doesn't move, and his fingers never withdraw.

"He…he met with Robert regularly for a short time," I admit, barely recognizing the sound of my own voice.

Mischa blinks, cold and collected once again. "How regularly?"

"Weekly at some points," I admit. "Every few months at others. It changed."

"That son of a bitch." He turns away from me, and I'm ignored in favor of the man whose face I can still clearly recall.

Black eyes. Dark curls. Younger than most. He smelled like cigar smoke and thick cologne I'd still taste on my tongue for weeks. Before the worst of the memories can descend, however, movement catches the corner of my eye. Mischa, reaching into his pocket. For his knife? No, a cell phone, I realize as my heart creeps to my throat. He dials a number quickly and brings it to his ear.

"This is Stepanov," he says into the receiver. "I'm calling a fucking meeting. Pecavi. Midnight. Bring them all." He hangs up, turning his attention back to me. "You want to earn another concession from me, Little One?" he wonders. But there is no mistake: it's not a question, and he doesn't offer kindness. "Then I'm going to need you to put that memory of yours to good fucking use. Or," he adds, sweeping his gaze along my body, "I'll utilize your pretty head in another way. Understood?"

I can only nod.

CHAPTER 18

"You claimed your husband never mentioned the *Mafiya* around you," Mischa questions as we advance through the corridor.

My steps are hesitant in his wake. I know enough of him to suspect that he doesn't divulge information like this willingly. No, his sudden talkativeness hides a more nefarious purpose: the first round of a brand-new game.

Do I want to play?

It's not like I have a choice.

"No," I admit cautiously. "He didn't."

"Should I enlighten you?"

I swallow hard, weighing the implications of such a suggestion. Does the twisted reason for my fate really matter?

"Ten families," he explains, making the decision for me, "each one with more wealth and power than your fucking Winthorps.

Together, we are united, under the guidance of one leader. In theory…"

A word springs to mind: *Pakhan.* Him?

"Twenty-four years ago, your husband's family started a war, Little One. I plan to end it, soon. Once and for all." His hands flex menacingly at his sides, the knuckles cracking in unison. "So do not make the mistake of assuming that, because you aren't dead now, I've changed my mind. In fact, I want you to tell me something."

"W-what?" I gather up the nerve to ask after seconds have passed, sensing that's what he wants: me to take the bait.

He continues past the door to his room and stops near the one beside it instead, heightening the foreboding tension building in my belly. "Think about how you want to die," Mischa commands as he opens the door.

I falter in the hall as my blood runs cold at the grim suggestion. He isn't joking.

Rather than demand an answer now, my murderer snatches my wrist and drags me over the threshold of the newer room. He switches a nearby light on, and with my thoughts stalled by terror, he pulls me in close, lowering his mouth near my ear. "So tell me, Ellen Winthorp. Strangulation? No…" He runs the fingers of his free hand along my tender throat and frowns. "You'd like that."

Would I? My lungs refuse to expand, and the sensation is anything but pleasurable. He could kill me like this easily: smothering my soul through nearness alone.

"What about a knife?" He sweeps his gaze along my chest as if hunting for the right place to strike. Eventually, his eyes settle over my rib cage and narrow thoughtfully. "I could make it slow, Little One."

His hand falls to his hip, and desperation makes my lips spring apart.

"G-gun," I rasp, naming Robert's preferred weapon. Whenever my husband eventually did tire of me, at least I knew for certain his method of choice. He'd dispose of me the same way he dispatched the animals he hunted: one bullet right between the eyes. Simple and clean, he'd say.

Mischa, however, frowns at the suggestion. "Shooting you." He shrugs as if considering it. Then he shakes his head and dips his fingers into his pocket, retrieving the hidden blade. "You aren't afraid of guns, Little One," he deduces musingly. "I've seen it. You aren't afraid of my hands, either. No…but the knife—" He raises the blade, brandishing it in the orange glow of the lamp. "This frightens you. Why?"

Hypnotized by the gleaming metal's edge, I can't answer him. Memories flash across my psyche too quickly to suppress: *pain, blood, so much blood.*

"You Winthorps and your knives." He brings the blade closer, positioning it toward my throat, and chuckles when I flinch. "This way." Nodding to himself, he steps back, returning the blade to his pocket. "Sit."

He gestures to the bed in the center of the room.

I sit on the edge of the mattress, and he stands over me without revealing a hint of what he has planned. I can't help the hesitant way my eyes trace the waistband of his pants. His hands remain open at his sides, but tension sizzles off him, prickling my skin.

"Are you afraid?" he wonders.

Am I? After a second's hesitation, I nod.

"You should be," he agrees, raking a hand along his scalp. "But… you *aren't.* Don't try to deny it. I've smelled fear on you before." His nostrils flare as if chasing that scent. Disappointed, he shrugs in disgust. "No. You are waiting. Watching. You still think you can survive."

"I don't." Once more, I question his assertions. The cunning woman he described sounds nothing like the Ellen Winthorp I know. "I-I—"

"I suppose I could threaten to kill you now, Little One." He pauses, letting the prospect linger while stoking my anxiety like flames. "But I might as well use you while I can. You said your husband never taught you how to gamble." His gaze roves over me, and with nothing to disguise my body's reaction, parts of me tighten. Stiffen. Heat. "I will make you a wager. Apart from your life, think of something you want from me."

"Huh?" I blink in confusion, unable to disguise the reaction before he notices. Something I want? *Mercy.*

As if aware of the desire, he chuckles again. "I know what I want from you. Fail me tonight and it's mine."

"And if I don't fail?" I'm not sure where the challenge came from. Why I even care. Men like him and Robert play their games with only one winner in mind.

Rather than reinforce that reality out loud, Mischa tilts his mouth in a wicked angle. "I'll humor you, Little One."

As he turns his back to me, I'm painfully aware that we're not in his room, but a new domain. This one is smaller, the furniture less ornate, the bed sheets a bloody shade of red. Rather than a dresser, there's a wardrobe tucked into the corner, which Mischa approaches. Beyond his shoulder, I only make out a swatch of colored fabric before he turns and tosses something onto the bed beside me.

"Put it on."

My fingers obediently clench the burgundy fabric. It's a dress. Thin. Small. Something sets it apart from the other skimpy items he gave me before though; it's finely tailored, comparable to what Briar would wear. This belonged to someone…

"Now," Mischa snaps.

Suppressing my questions, I draw the gown over my head, surprised by the modest length and plunging neckline.

"Forget Robert Winthorp," he warns. He runs his fingers through my hair, flicking the strands forward to cover most of my face. "Tonight, you are *mine*." He captures my chin in his grip and roughly runs his thumb over the healing wounds on my left cheek. Then he withdraws something from his pocket. Flat. Square. A bandage large enough to cover the worst of the cuts. Satisfied, he draws back, observing me from afar.

"Get some of that sleep you crave, Little One," he commands, heading for the door. "Tonight, you better be willing to place your bets."

⁂

*L*eft alone in the strange room, I notice nothing worth examining—at first. It's slightly smaller than his, with an adjacent bathroom composed of white marble instead of black. The bedsheets feel stiff, unslept in. There are few baubles or mementos on the nightstands and the lone vanity, just like in his room.

The wardrobe is another matter, however. The moment I open the doors, a scent rushes out to greet me. Sweet. Soft. Feminine. It lingers in every piece of clothing I find. Most are elegant gowns like the one Mischa picked for me, but tucked behind them, I find simpler garments. A blouse. A skirt. The style is older than the bright fashions Briar prefers, more modest. They're far from what Robert would choose for me, as well.

But Mischa? Was his woman this modest creature who preferred emerald silk and soft tweed?

I try to picture her, someone who could pique his interest in ways other than a hateful fuck. Only the haziest image comes to mind. Brown eyes, maybe? Someone taller, perhaps. The doomed Anna-Natalia?

Removing the clothing in question reveals no answers. I don't find her when I carefully shed my red dress in favor of one from the wardrobe. It fits me, which is the first surprise. The second is how lovingly it's been preserved. No one has worn them in a very long time, yet the fabric maintains its shape.

What are you doing, Ellen?

My subconscious haunts me as I approach the vanity. I almost don't recognize the person I find looking back. Her eyes aren't as empty as I'm used to. Something lurks there. Pain? Or a more dangerous, obscure emotion that would never take root in my husband's domain?

Curiosity.

Mischa's woman doesn't reveal herself, even in the drawers or the neat arrangement of items placed before the round mirror. Pink lipstick. A small vial of perfume. A silver brush. My fingers settle over each item individually, seeking any clue of their previous owner. I don't find a ghost. Just a strange, impulsive need to drag the brush through my tangled hair and swipe my lips with the lipstick. The perfume is the most dangerous item of all to disturb. I know that even before I spray a hint of it against my wrist, inhaling the feminine scent.

Who was this ghost who smelled of roses?

Trembling with apprehension, I shed the clothing and return it to the wardrobe. Then I redress myself in the red slip, climb onto the bed and wait. Sleep should be a tempting offer without Mischa there to haunt my every moment, but my eyes refuse to close. My heart refuses to still.

Instead, I breathe in shallowly and count the seconds as they pass. I wait, lingering in my monster's shadow. This room disguises his scent too well and I'm left inhaling a stranger—two of them. One is bloodied and broken, the wife of a distant villain. The other is an enigma, lingering in the home of an even worse creature.

And she didn't even bother to leave her secrets behind.

The moment my eyes finally begin to drift shut, Mischa comes for me. I startle to awareness and find him in the doorway, gesturing with a silent wave of his hand for me to follow.

Together, we return to the entryway of the manor, and I sense a drastic change in the atmosphere. Unease. It lingers as he marches through an archway opposite the one toward the dining room. Noises echo, betraying a flurry of unseen activity. Voices. Chaos. Suddenly, a man appears at the end of the hallway.

"There you are." Vanya approaches, wearing a black collared shirt and pants instead of the gray fatigues. He nods once when he sees me before turning his attention to Mischa. He eyes his leader warily, lowering his voice. "Are you sure about this? On such short notice?"

He's anxious, but if Mischa feels the same his posture reveals nothing. He's stoic, his jaw set in a grim line of determination.

"I am done playing the role of mediator," he says. "It's time we fucking fight for what we want. Those who refuse to fall in line can grapple with the consequences."

"You know most of them will follow you," Vanya agrees. "But Sergei—"

"I can handle him," Mischa interjects. "But can you? You made your choice to stay by my side, not his. Tell me now if you regret it?"

Vanya frowns, eyeing something far beyond this conversation only he can see. Finally, he shakes his head. "No."

"Good." Mischa squares his shoulders, continuing down the hall.

He wants to say more, I can tell. Something personal. Whatever it is, the words never leave his throat, and Vanya continues in the opposite direction.

"You're losing already, Little One," Mischa warns. He snatches my wrist, drawing me to his side. "You are mine, remember?"

It's one role I don't know how to emulate, ironically. Robert thought of me as his trophy. His wife. *His* prize. Mischa seems to expect a certain demeanor. Maybe the answer lurks in the heated way he uttered those words. *You are mine.*

But how does one display the ownership of a beast? It's a trick question. Monsters never possess their victims. They rip them apart. Devour. Destroy. Then they lord over the mangled pieces.

He already has me hanging together by a thread. I'm not prideful enough to deny it. I can sense my soul splintering around me with every passing second that his heat leeches into my skin.

There was a reason Robert never gambled. "Only fools with nothing worth having risk it all," he smugly claimed.

He was the son of a wealthy businessman with the world at his fingertips, after all. What use did he have for something as elusive as hope and luck?

I'm not even half as secure as he is, yet I still can't make the leap. So I eye the floor of the hallway and count the steps we take until Mischa finally pulls me to a stop. We're in a larger room I don't recognize. A polished floor stretches beneath a vaulted ceiling with scattered fixtures casting intermittent light. A meeting room?

There's a table in the center, like the makeshift one at the safe house where Boris haggled for me. More men fill this room, however. At least ten are seated around the table, with more lurking behind them, flooding nearly every available space. At a glance, the group appears homogenous, but on a second appraisal, it's easy to see the subtle divides that separate some groups from the others. Of the ten men seated, each one seems to command a section of the room wherein those gathered are facing him. Some are wearing suits. Others are wearing casual fatigues like Mischa. One man is even lounging in a simple tee shirt and jeans, smirking at those around him.

As Mischa approaches the remaining chair, a hush falls. Behind us, numerous footsteps echo in unison. His men, spearheaded by Vanya.

"So, Stepanov," one of the men says, seizing the attention as Mischa sits. He's older, his eyes piercing and narrowed. He glances Mischa over with barely concealed disgust, but there's respect in how he inclines his head toward him, even as he spits his words out. "You called us here. For what? To join in your insane fucking plan—"

"To talk," Mischa says, effortlessly cutting over him though he never raises his voice.

I find myself biting my lower lip in recognition of one tool I've only ever seen Winthorp men possess so freely: *power.*

It's in the way he holds his head. How his shoulders convey a fearless grace. He's not the oldest man here, or the biggest, or even the handsomest. But no one can keep their eyes off him for very long.

"To talk?" another man wonders, his accent thick and indiscernible. "Or to beg for help in your fucking war with Winthorp—"

"Show some respect," another man interjects, dark-haired and solidly built. His eyes hold an eerie sense of calm that negates the impatience of the other two men vying to speak above him. "Nikolaus. Yohan. You forget your place before your *Pakhan.*"

That word has the effect of a whip. The two men stiffen in their seats. Their glares remain, but they hold their tongues.

"Now, Mischa," the calmer man says, meeting his gaze from across the table. "We're listening."

"It's time we head off the Winthorps at the fucking head," Mischa declares, his voice reverberating to the farthest reaches of the room. "And I don't speak out of some petty fucking feud," he adds. "This is about survival."

"Survival?" Nikolaus, the older man, scoffs. "You mean *greed*. There have been rumors, *Pakhan*. That you went after the man himself. Robert. His daughter. Considering the little bitch is on her honeymoon with one of the most powerful money lenders in the world, I presume that you miscalculated."

"I did lead an attack on her," Mischa admits without a shred of shame. "Robert was prepared. He used a decoy. Some disposable toy of his son's." He shrugs with a malicious jerk of his shoulder. "I gave her to my men and left her body for the bastard to find—"

"And found yourself a distraction, I see," Nikolaus snidely interjects, turning his attention to me. He sneers in disgust at what little of my face he can see through the curtain of my hair. "You're getting more blatant, Mischa—"

"Show some respect," another man cuts in, forcefully slamming his hand over the table.

"Enough." Mischa sits forward, his smile dismissive. "This bitch is more than a distraction." He grabs my wrist, tugging me closer to the table, until I have no choice but to sit on his lap.

The other men tense, warily watching the display. He's never brought a woman to their meetings before, I suspect. Not like this. His arm possessively encircles my waist from behind, but there's tension coiled into every strip of muscle. A warning, broadcasted solely to me. *Play your role, Little One.*

"She's more like a lucky charm. She's skilled at spotting liars, you see. *Traitors*."

The way he stresses that word sends a ripple of unease throughout the room. Through one man in particular. My eyes go to him automatically, though I'm not sure why at first. He is standing just beyond the table, his face partially hidden by shadow. But his shape is familiar.

"Should I explain?" Mischa's fingers trail my cheek, turning my face toward him. The look in his eyes takes my breath away: hot, molten anger. For me? No… For once, his ire has a new target. "Show them, Little One," he goads. "You think there are any traitors in our midst?"

With his thumb pressing forcefully against my bottom lip, I sense what he doesn't say out loud once again: *Here's your chance. So, gamble.*

"Is this a game to you?" Nikolaus demands, his irritation visibly echoed by at least six of the other seated men. "Just who are you trying to accuse, *Pakhan*—"

"I don't know," Mischa says, his voice deceptively soft. "Just who among us would dare betray our families. Our blood. Our lives?"

With each word, his volume rises while a hush simultaneously falls over the assembled crowd. Out of shock. Disbelief.

"I suppose that you have more than some 'lucky' whore to bring charges against someone, *Pakhan*," the calmer man wonders.

"What do you think?" Mischa tilts my chin down toward him. "Do you sense a fucking liar, Little One?"

Slowly, my gaze drifts across the room to the man in Nikolaus's section. He's moved deeper into the ranks, almost as if attempting to stay out of view. But I can smell him even from here; there is no escaping memory.

"Kostas!" Mischa declares warmly, zoning in on the same shadowed figure. "Come closer, brother."

"Mischa—" Nikolaus rises to his feet with both hands braced against the table. "You wouldn't dare accuse my son."

Several murmurs of concern rise, creating a chorus. *You're crossing a dangerous line.*

Mischa smiles, revealing nothing. "Let's hear it from the man himself," he declares, beckoning Kostas closer with a wave of his hand. "You wouldn't dare consort with an enemy, now would you, brother?"

Gradually, Kostas comes forward to stand behind his father, and I can't fight the instinctive tensing of my muscles. He hasn't changed much since his last meeting with Robert. Except for the fact that he's lost his mocking smile.

"You have a pretty little bitch," he mused once about me, his accent crisp and American. "She's almost as sexy as that sister of yours."

Robert, ever the businessman, laughed at the insult to me. Right before he formed a fist and punched the younger man's jaw for the insult to his sister. Blood was everything to a Winthorp. The blood they deemed worth protecting, anyway.

Mischa's words keep echoing through my thoughts. *You don't know a damn thing about your fucking Winthorp.*

"What is the reason for this, Mischa?" Kostas wonders, drawing me back to the present. His scowl betrays the same apparent lack of respect his father has. But, as his eyes flicker across me, they widen ever so slightly.

"Have you seen this whore before?" Mischa wonders, tilting my face in the other man's direction.

Kostas scoffs dismissively. "I don't remember every bitch I've fucked, *Pakhan*."

Mischa just chuckles. "This one remembers *you*." He casually flicks a strand of hair behind my ear, exposing more of my face. "She was a particular favorite of Robert Winthorp, the younger. Do you remember now?"

Chaos erupts.

Reddening with rage, Nikolaus nearly lunges across the table. "You've crossed a line, *Mal'chik*."

"Have I?" Mischa wonders.

This close to him, I feel the subtle changes in his body before they unfold across his face. The dangerous tensing. The faint flames of rage prickling against my skin.

"Then let me ask him directly. Kostas…have you been selling to Robert Winthorp?"

Redness blossoms over the younger man's cheeks. "You even have to ask?" But his eyes cut in my direction again, slower this time. In recognition. His throat bobs slightly as he swallows. "I'd never—"

"I assume you have your personal accountant on call," Mischa says over him, directing the question to his father. "Have him run these numbers through your accounts. See if any holes match." He fishes the crumpled notebook page out of his pocket and shoves it toward Nikolaus.

The older man sneers and then spits at the table. "How fucking dare you."

Mischa doesn't display any hint of regret. Instead, his smile turns feral around the edges, his eyes less mocking than before. "If you don't want your son's treason to reflect badly on you, Nikolaus, then I suggest you run the goddamn numbers."

For a tense few seconds, they eye each other with only the polished sliver of wood between them. Then Nikolaus snatches the page up and hands it off to one of the men behind him. "Do it," he commands. "And when my son is vindicated, I will demand more than blood in compensation for sullying my family's name."

Mischa nods as if to convey, *As you wish*, though he radiates tension like a furnace. Each wave of quiet, smoldering anger feels different from the rage he directs at me. It's colder. Harder. Terrifying. Being this close to him is like having the veil that usually shielded off my emotions ripped away. I feel it all. Fear. Uncertainty. Anger?

Survival.

Think, Ellen. My memories contain a different detail about Kostas, beyond something as intangible as money. Without giving myself the time to rethink the action, I lower my mouth to Mischa's ear. His jaw clenches at my nearness. The visible disgust is almost enough to make me flinch back in fear. Almost. Before I do, I whisper something so quickly that I fear for a second he misheard me.

He narrows his eyes further, processing the hurried words. Then...he throws his head back and laughs. "If your son won't come clean, Nikolaus, then perhaps we can settle another way?" He nods toward the younger man's waist. "The woman claims to remember something about your son. Something personal. Should I tell everyone just what that is?"

"I could have fucked that bitch from anywhere," Kostas snarls.

"Oh, but you couldn't have…" Mischa stands, jostling me from his lap and rising to his full height. Nikolaus may be taller, but it's clear who has the upper hand: Mischa isn't the one forced to bow in reverence.

"Do you want to know why?" Mischa pulls me closer. "Look at her face. Look closely. You couldn't have met this whore anywhere else because, as of four days ago, she belonged to Robert Winthorp."

"How can you know that?" the dark-haired man wonders, standing as well. His expression is more curious than hostile as he scans my face. He blinks. Frowns. Leans closer. There's a slight tilt to his mouth, betraying an emotion I struggle to name. Recognition? "The Winthorps wouldn't sell one of their women to you—"

"Because I'm the one who ripped her from his grip," Mischa says. "Isn't that right, Kostas?"

The younger man says nothing, his jaw clenched, his eyes blazing.

"And even if you don't believe me, can you tell me how she knows that you have a butterfly tattoo on your right hip?"

"I will not stand for this!" Nikolaus brandishes a fist, his voice booming. "How dare you—"

"Well, does he?" the dark-haired man interjects.

Nikolaus sputters. "S-Sergei?"

"Do you, boy?" Sergei presses, turning to Kostas.

"I… I…" The younger man can't even get a word out in his defense.

Not that Mischa seems to need one. "Run the numbers," he says. "If they are off by even a cent, I'll step down right fucking now. But if not…"

The murderous tone has the effect of casting a hush over the room again, thicker and heavier than any brief silence before it.

"If not, I demand retribution—"

"N-no," Nikolaus says, visibly deflating. His shoulders slump, his eyes widening with horror. "He is *my* son. *Pakhan*—"

"We put it to a vote," Sergei says, gesturing to the men around him. "If what the *Pakhan* says is true…then I second his suggestion. This would be beyond treason." His voice betrays an unsteady note: the only hint as to the rage lurking beneath his otherwise calm exterior. "The *Pakhan* should decide his punishment."

"No!" Nikolaus glances from man to man, searching for an ally among the sea of faces.

Two men nod solemnly in agreement, but they are vastly outnumbered by the quiet consensus. Before the decision can be reinforced out loud, however, one of the men behind Nikolaus taps his shoulder and hands him the slip of notebook paper. The look on his face is grim.

Without even waiting for the results to be read out loud, Mischa nods and two of his men circle the table for Kostas.

Before they can reach him, Nikolaus stands protectively before his son. "This…this is a setup," he snarls. "Revenge. How dare you——"

"Nikolaus," Sergei says sternly. "I suggest you use your head."

"Yes," Mischa says coldly. "I don't want to declare your entire family as my enemy. Step aside."

For several tense seconds, Nikolaus doesn't move as Mischa's men close in. Finally…he concedes, stepping back. Mischa's men, including Vanya, grab Kostas on either side and muscle him toward the back of the room.

Punishment. I shiver at Mischa's interpretation of the word.

"I suggest we end this meeting here, *Pakhan*," Sergei says, inclining his head respectfully. "This is more than enough excitement for one day." He eyes me once more before turning and marshaling the men loyal to him into action.

"Dismissed," Mischa says before exiting the room pulling me along after him.

My heart hammers a painful rhythm as he hauls me out into the hallway and through the rest of the house. He takes me directly to his room at the top of the stairs, closing the door behind us.

"You gambled big for your first time, Little One," he says, his voice low and grated. Here, the tension he wore like a cloak downstairs gradually reveals the exhaustion lurking underneath. His shoulders relax from their tense line, his jaw less hard.

The subtle changes aren't enough to humanize him though. Not even a little. But they keep my surging pulse at bay. I can breathe, at least.

"As promised, I'll uphold my end." He faces me, half in shadow. "Ask something of me, Little One. What do you want?"

It's a dare more than it is a legitimate question. He's curious. It's almost enough to counteract his earlier rage. Almost.

"I won't release you, of course," he adds. "But...tell me."

It should be impossible to settle on one thing. He won't uphold any request—I know that. Yet my mind hovers over a million different things I could ask. Tempting things. Irrelevant things. Before those thoughts can even take hold, reality shoves its way to the forefront.

"The girl," I say, picturing the waif from Nicolai's. "Don't sell her, regardless of what you do to me..."

I trail off as Mischa laughs. He throws his head back, choking out the vicious, hollow sound. It's still echoing on the air as he fixes the brunt of his gaze in my direction.

"You really thought I'd go so far as to sell a *child*, Little One?" Another laugh escapes him, sharper than the first. "The girl didn't ask for this. I have no reason to sell her. But you..." He approaches me, running his hand along my injured cheek once he's close enough. "*You* have a wealth of sins to atone for, Robert Winthorp's wife. Your fate is far beyond any mercy I could spare."

It's surprisingly easy to accept my death sentence when it's uttered so finally. Mischa doesn't draw out his torture in games and riddles. He murmurs the truth into my ear and watches me tremble.

"What else?" His thumb nudges my chin, tilting it upright. "Ask."

There's more than a mocking curiosity tainting his tone now. There's impatience. Desperation? He wants something to take his mind off of what happened below, I suspect.

Licking my lips, I spit out the first thing to come to mind. "Tell me. Was it really you? At Winthorp manor that night?"

"I won't humor a fantasy," Mischa warns. "Ask me something else."

"I…" I rack my brain and settle on a pathetic whim. "Can you call me by my name?" The plea sounds so breathless when voiced out loud. My name. Not bitch, or whore, or Little One, or Robert Winthorp's wife.

"Ellen?" Mischa wonders, drawing hard on the syllables. "What does your husband call you?"

I have to force the name off the tip of my tongue. "Elle."

"Elle," he echoes, tasting it. "Is that what you want *me* to call you?"

"No." I cringe at the thought. Robert's word, here. No. Even Mischa's brutality couldn't erase the dark memories clinging to it.

"Then what?" He's even closer, his breath scalding my tender cheek.

"I… My mother called me Rose." I didn't mean to tell him that. A part of me despairs at having let something so sacred slip. "B-but you don't have to—"

"Rose." His nostrils flare as if inhaling the name itself. "Is that what you want me to call you?"

No, a part of me whispers. Rose is beautiful. Rose is untouched. Rose is one of the few parts of me Robert never desecrated.

"Fine *Rose*," Mischa says after nearly a minute goes by without a response. He lets his hand fall but doesn't back away. If anything, his heat soaks through the fabric of my dress, assaulting me just as brutally as his knife did. "Now, I want something from you."

My breath catches in my throat. "Y-yes?"

"Your husband. Do you love him?"

"Yes." My answer is more instinctive than anything. Loving Robert is akin to how I feel most people would categorize worshiping their God—at least the one the Winthorp's chosen priest described.

Robert was all knowing in my world. All powerful. He protected me when he felt the urge and punished me when he thought I deserved it. My life was ruled by his whims, and it was all I knew.

"Good." Mischa nods in approval. "It should make it easier to die for him."

"Does it?" Once again, words sprang from my lips without my soul's permission. "No one decides how they die."

Or anyone else's death, for that matter. Robert controlled my life. I'd always assumed he'd planned it down to the very end. And now?

There are blank pages hidden in the twisted book he wrote for me. While Mischa dictates the narrative, I have some control over what goes on every page. Some say in the final chapter of my story.

"The man, Kostas?" I ask, once again speaking without permission. "Will you kill him?"

Mischa's eyes lose what little patience they had, turning hard like flint. "I suggest you don't trouble yourself with Kostastantin Vorshev," he warns. "In fact, Rose…Vorshev should be the very least of your worries."

My heart races, pounding against my rib cage. Hearing him call me "Little One" is chilling enough. But *Rose?* His lethal cadence sharpens the name, transforming it into a weapon more than a moniker.

"Do you know what you've seen tonight?" he asks, his voice still dipping toward that alarmingly low octave. "Do you?"

I shake my head, even as my mind spits out what few adjectives describe it. Ten groups of men gathered together who, for the most part, deferred to him. What is that word he said before? *Mafiya.*

"Every last soul in that room wants your husband dead, Little One," he tells me, running his fingers through my hair without warning. "And not only that. They want his head on a pike, your family name ruined. You have no idea, do you?" He looks into my eyes and frowns at what he sees. "Even Vanya. He's not as innocent as he seems. Once, he was in my position so don't doubt for a second that he couldn't return to his old ways if given enough incentive. The Winthorps killed his daughter, after all."

He waits, watching as his words sink into my skull.

"You want to know what happened the night you think you saw me? A young fuck-up had been on a mission to claim the next victim in the feud. Thirteen. And he failed. But I haven't. You will pay the price for Anna's life," he declares. "She was the sole heir to the Vasilev name, niece of its head, Sergei. You haven't heard his name, either?" He chuckles, low in his throat as if amused by the absurdity of it all. "Oh, I'm sure your husband knows. He may seem collected now, but Sergei was a million times worse than I am, Little One. During his prime, he would have gutted you without hesitation, and so much worse. I can tell you for a fact that *he* wouldn't be fooled by your little stunts—" He breaks off, his eyes narrowing at his use of the phrase.

By accident?

"And neither am I." He shakes his head fiercely and grits his teeth together so hard that I hear them crack. "Sergei wreaked hell over the Winthorps. I will finish what he started." There's admiration in his tone. There's some disgust as well, lurking deep where I doubt he even realizes it. "You are nowhere near the prize Briar would have been. But your husband seems to want you back. The question is: How badly?"

Me? No, Robert wants his numbers back. His dutiful wife. His willing victim. So many titles are tied to me, personally. Yet here I am. Still captive. Still Mischa's.

Does that reality dishearten me? Or comfort me?

"Don't look so excited," Mischa warns. "I've been wondering why he let you go so fucking easily if he's willing to kill to have you back. Is he that confident I won't kill you? Or does he have that much trust in you?"

Heat prickles through my skin as he advances, backing my body into the wall with his sheer presence alone. I taste his flavor on my tongue, unwanted and unbidden. Salt. Musk. No Vodka, however. He wanted to be sharp tonight. For the meeting? Or to finally put an end to his game?

"T-trust?" I echo, playing along.

His nostrils flare in triumph and he nods. "Oh, yes," he murmurs. "You have Vanya wrapped around your finger—he begged me not to kill you. Did he tell you?"

I swallow hard. Is he lying? I want to assume so, but his eyes are too dark. Confused. "N-no," I croak. "He didn't."

"Your husband must have trained you well," Mischa admits. "I saw how Kostas looked at you, though I can tell that you didn't choose him for yourself. Did he make you, hmm? Your precious Robert?"

He pauses for an answer I don't bother to give. I can't.

"And yet, you *love* him," he reiterates, lowering his mouth near my throat as if to taste my pulse through my skin. "Describe it for me, Little Rose. How does a man like that earn your love?"

"W-what?" My thoughts run together and collide, thrown into turmoil by the question. "He is my husband—"

"That's not what I asked." He lunges, grinding his weight into me with more menace than any weapon could ever inflict.

I want to run. I want to shove him off and risk his anger. But I can't; my arms stay woodenly at my sides, paralyzed by his heat.

"When he touches you, what do you feel?"

He cups my breast through the silk of my gown. What do I feel? Fire.

"Does he make you scream, Little One? Do you come around his cock as easily as you do around mine?"

Too…dangerous. My mind shies from the mocking taunt, but there is no escape from him. No escape from the memories haunting me—not Robert. Just him. Wrecking, violent, unbearable *him.*

"If I were a good man, I would just kill you," he breathes out almost as if to himself more than to me. "But I'm not. Am I, Little Rose? I want your husband to suffer more than just your death." The words come in growled snippets. It's like he's thinking up the plan as he goes, embellishing his own twisted ending. "I'm going to break you…" He brings his massive hands to my skull, cupping both sides of my face. Bit by bit, he applies enough pressure to make me wince. "I'll exorcize him from your head, Little One. I'll rip him from you until there's nothing left."

It's a heated promise. A threat. And he means every word.

So why does a part of me sigh in relief?

<h1 style="text-align:center">CHAPTER 19</h1>

A world without Robert. Would I even survive such a reality?

The answer is simple: *no*. Which is the only damn reason why Mischa suddenly seems so eager to replace my husband.

Robert Winthorp *is* my identity. Without him, Ellen is a hollow shell with enough space for a new monster to infest.

"Killing you would be too easy," Mischa muses, lowering his head enough to pierce my shrinking bubble of personal space. "No…"

I jump as a fiery line of heat traces the edge of my windpipe: his *tongue* stealing away the gasp building in my throat.

"You deserve worse than that."

"W-why?" I instantly regret challenging him—a sharp, warning bite on my collar is his retribution.

Only *he* can do this to me: make me question despite the consequences. Make me disobey every instinct in my body urging me to do the opposite. Run. Scream. *Survive.*

"Because your sins are so much greater than that fucker's." He presses my skull tighter between his palms, breathing heavily into my skin. Lust mingles with the hate, a familiar, stomach-churning scent even he can't disguise. "You *love* him. You accept that evil, twisted fuck. Don't you?"

I can't escape the suspicion that he wants me to deny it. His eyes glint, illuminated by an emotion I'm unable to name. A part of me hazards a guess anyway and my stomach clenches in foreboding. *Jealousy?*

"You do," he deduces before I can answer. "Fine. Since you have no problem sharing your bed with a fucking monster, you should have no problem accepting me."

He grabs my arm and shoves me toward the bed. My back hits the mattress, leaving me looking up as he advances, his head bowed with predatory intent.

Fear shoots through my veins, stealing my breath away, even as my legs drift apart despite every instinct screaming at me to run. *You're afraid…*

"My Little Rose," Mischa murmurs, gritting the words out through clenched teeth. His gaze hungrily sweeps over my splayed limbs and the skewed dress. "Should I crush you all at once? Or rip you apart, petal by petal?"

The poetic language is a new weapon in his arsenal. It's devastating. I'm paralyzed as he uses his knee to nudge my legs farther apart, creating enough space for him to fit in between them.

With slow, deliberate motions, he tugs at his waistband but grunts in disapproval when I begin to stare. "Eyes up here. I want you to look at *me*. I want to see him die in your eyes."

Eyes. As commanded, I meet his gaze and hold it. I fracture beneath the strength of it. His deepen to a shade unlike any I've ever seen. Endless amber. Fathomless. *God.* Ripples of tension release all over my body, making me quake against the sheets. They still reek of our combined scents. Blood and sweat. Harsh and soft. The conflicting aromas flood my nostrils as the rasp of an unraveling zipper pierces the air.

"I want you to think of him." The request resonates down my spine as his silhouette flickers in the shadows, suddenly looming larger. Closer. "I want him in your head when I fuck you."

Think of him. That's impossible. For the first time in so long, Robert isn't here, and the silence left behind is deafening. A new man fills the abandoned space, his pupils pinprick as his body effortlessly mounts mine, his face coming within inches of my own.

Heavy hands palm my waist, wrenching the hem of my dress up, revealing me bare underneath.

"Look at me, Little Rose," Mischa hisses, his voice raspy, his gaze almost unbearable to meet head-on.

A heartbeat later I feel him: running his fingers between my legs before replacing them with something thicker. Harder. Pulsating.

Then…

One thrust takes him deep, jarring him closer, his nose brushing mine, his groan uttered against my parted lips. My eyes flutter shut as sensation floods my entire being. The world fades for a brief, cruel moment and I'm alone inside my body, even as he dominates it. God, the way he feels. It's. Unlike. Anything. Else.

My thoughts scatter. I can only piece them back together in snippets. Full. Need. More.

"Fuck, *look at me*." His eyes are heavy-lidded when I do. His teeth seize his bottom lip as he rears back on his knees, slipping his hands beneath me for enough leverage to control the depth of every thrust. Deep. Deeper. Deeply.

My head lolls—I'm a slave to every frantic motion.

"Should I tell your husband how fucking wet you feel, Little One?" he grunts out, yanking me closer. "How your eyes roll back into your fucking head when you come. The sounds you make…"

I can't. My eyes squeeze shut, blocking out his face, chiseled with concentration. He snarls in anger, and I feel his cock stiffen—thicker, harder.

"I told you to look at me." His nails pierce the flesh of my hips in a warning. "Look at me, Little Rose."

I hear the threat of punishment in his voice. Still, I shut my eyes tighter. It's an act I'd never perform with Robert. I'd *never* disobey him. I'd never tremble at the brutality as anger takes over his movements, driving him even deeper. Into my head. Into my goddamn soul.

I'd never relish the violation.

But Mischa makes me speak a new language composed of frantic, whispered words.

"Please…p-please—"

"What?" He pauses, still buried to the hilt, leaving little room to suck in enough air to speak. "Please what?"

What? Those words won't come. I have to show him. My trembling fingers poorly convey what I want—*need*. They brush my breast in a timid stroke.

"You want me to touch you?" Mischa wonders, barely intelligible. "Beg me to."

I just nod, smothering my moan into the sheets as his thick, callused fingers graze my skin beneath the plunging neckline of my dress. He doesn't touch me. He violates me, clenching flesh and squeezing to the point of bruising. It hurts, drawing a gasp from my lips. It…feels.

My nerves can't resist him the way years of abuse trained them against Robert. His warmth sinks into my skin, his callused flesh grating over mine and melting any hint of resistance. The pinpricks of pain meld with the friction of him still inside me, churning my insides to mush and melting every sane thought in my head.

Mischa grates out something that isn't English, capturing my nipple between his thumb and his forefinger, guiding it to a stiff point. Then even words cease to matter. Our language becomes a series of groans and gasps smothered into silk and skin. His fingers roam without care or reason, fanning over my rib cage, plunging through my hair, and grasping strands so hard that my eyes water.

"Look at me." His teeth find my earlobe, grinding it between them. "Fuck. *Look at me.*"

I do. And the sight of his face, hard with determination, steals my breath away.

He looks too powerful. Too real. Too raw, hungry for me.

He crushes me with his last thrust, refusing to shift his weight even as he empties himself into me. I'm trapped beneath him, forced to bear every lethal pound. It's almost as if he's trying to drive Robert out through his presence alone.

I try to hang on to that familiar monster. I try…

But, with every passing second, his evil is harder to grasp, like smoke chased away by a raging inferno.

And, without his protection, I'm devoured whole.

CHAPTER 20

I wake up twisted in black sheets that smell of musk and sweat. For a brief, dangerous moment, I forget. My eyes flutter open as I expect what I'll see: a view of my suite at Winthorp manor. Breakfast should be coming soon, Robert soon after. Resigned, I turn toward the door—but white walls don't greet me. Then the hum of a man's deep, unsteady breathing rips the fantasy away once and for all.

Not Robert.

He always let me recollect myself in peace. He never *watched* over me in my sleep, his gaze searing my skin.

"I know you're awake," Mischa says after nearly a full minute of silence, his voice gruff. "Get up."

I dutifully roll onto my side, taking in more of my surroundings. He left me slung over the edge of the bed with my feet against the floor. I still feel his release drying against my inner thigh, along with his taste on my tongue. A flicker of motion from the corner of my eye reveals him standing near the opposite side of the bed, fully dressed.

"Here." He lets something fall beside me onto the bed and offers an object clenched in his hand: a glass of water. "Swallow it."

Swallow? Groaning, I muster my sore limbs enough to sit upright as my hand feels over the sheets. Something small and round strikes my fingers. White. A pill? "W-what is it?" I risk asking, my voice hoarse.

Could he have devised some new plan to use me against Robert? Drug me? Poison?

He doesn't provide an answer for so long that my muscles start to protest from the awkward position. Is it a test? Or maybe something so much worse, I realize, looking up. His eyes are narrowed, his jaw clenched against a response.

"My plan doesn't include sending you back to your husband pregnant," he says finally.

Oh. The pill in my hand takes on a less nefarious purpose. I swallow it diligently and sip from the glass he's shoved into my hand. This action raises a question I don't have the nerve to voice: Why now? Only days ago, he scoffed at the idea of contraception.

Has he decided to extend his timeline for my capture? When put into perspective with my inevitable death, I'm not sure what's more appealing: dying sooner or later?

"I think you played your role too well last night, Little Rose," Mischa adds, frowning. "You caught more notice than I expected." His hand brushes my bandaged cheek and I recoil. The touch almost felt genuine. Unconcerned, Mischa curls his fingers into a fist instead. "Someone offered to buy you. They offered me *a lot* to buy you."

"You still plan to sell me," I deduce, folding my hands together.

Suddenly, his previous action makes perfect sense. Am I surprised? Disappointed? At least he saw the value in ensuring he only has one life to take when he finally tires of me. How noble.

"Who said anything about selling you?" Mischa wonders, tilting my chin toward him. "Oh, no, Robert's wife. I am not finished with you yet."

But... I sense a big one, even as the seconds pass without him saying it.

He scans my face with renewed interest. Something is on his mind. Something pressing enough to supposedly make him overlook accepting money for me. At least for now.

"You said Marnie was your mother."

It's surprisingly difficult, hearing her name come out of his mouth. His accent distorts the two beautiful syllables I've only heard uttered inside my head for so long.

"Y-yes—"

"When were you born?"

"She died when I was seven," I admit, skirting the question directly. Why? I don't know. He's asking for too much. More than Robert ever has. More than anyone.

"Which makes you twenty-three," he says, deducing my age for himself. "You are younger than I thought, Little Rose." He genuinely seems surprised, and I can't resist attempting to gauge his age as well.

His skin is weathered by more than just scars. Hard, long years. Brutal years. If someone put a gun to my head, I'd peg him to be around his mid-thirties, the same age as Robert.

He never reveals the number himself, however. Instead, he cocks his head, observing me even more closely. "I suppose it makes sense now," he says, almost to himself. "You must look like her. Perhaps he wanted to finish the job."

"W-who?" I don't know where the courage to voice the question comes from. "Who wanted to buy me?"

"A dangerous man, Little Rose," he admits. "Whoever told you that story about your mother lied to you. Or you've been lying to *me*—"

"No," I say, risking his anger to cut him off. "I'd never lie about her."

"Well, she didn't 'leave' Winthorp Manor before you were born," he says. "She was taken—no, she was *marked*."

"You mean…" I reach up automatically, feeling my brand sting beneath a layer of gauze. "My mother?" A part of this feud? It seems too fanatical. Too convoluted, even for the Winthorps.

And yet…

For the first time, Mischa doesn't sport either his mocking smirk or his hostile glare. "It seems I have much to teach you, Little Rose," he says softly, drawing his hand away. "I am not your only enemy. Not by far. In fact"—he rubs his chin while an unreadable expression shapes his features—"I'll leave the choice up to you. I won't bind you or lock you away tonight. You may have full run of the property to stick your nose where it doesn't belong. And I hope you remember what lurks beyond my protection."

"P-protection?"

It's the first time he's phrased my captivity in that way: *protection.* Mangled by his accent, the word sounds more like doom than salvation.

"Perhaps." His lip quirks in a dangerous imitation of a smile—or a grimace. "I don't want to break you just yet. Your death should mean something, Little Rose. I want it to count. I want you to know full well when and why your blood is being spilled. All in good time."

He pulls away before I can see his expression. I have to discern what little clues I can from his stance. His shoulders harbor tension, his spine rigid. He's serious. He means it—and something warns me that he's thinking over my eventual death very carefully.

In a sick way, he almost reminds me of Briar as she planned her wedding, pouring her attention into every tiny detail to distract herself from the overall picture: that she was marrying a man her father had chosen and what dress she would wear or salad she selected didn't mean a damn thing in the grand scheme.

I don't know what's worse, really: being a slave to the whims of others or believing that, even for a second, you can somehow shape the narrative. That you have say. Maybe that's one small part of Robert I admire. Apart from sex, he never planned a damn thing. He took, and he fucked, and he let the cards lie where they may.

He never left me guessing.

"Has Ivan asked you about your mother?" Mischa asks.

I shake my head. "No."

"Lie to him if he does."

I can't stop myself from questioning, "Why?"

"Should I tell you?" He cocks his head, glancing at me over his shoulder. "No, I don't think I should," he decides. "But I suggest you trust me on this, Little Rose. Vanya is a good man"—he frowns as if annoyed by that fact—"but good men can have their own secrets."

With that, he heads for the door and shoulders it open, leaving my head spinning and more questions on my tongue. This time, I don't have the energy to voice them.

"I'll say this again: Have your run of the property," Mischa calls from the doorway. "Explore to your heart's content and remember how many monsters are hungry for you beyond these walls."

The door slams behind him, rattling the ornate frame surrounding it.

And I just sit here on my captor's bed, drowning in his scent.

Explore. The guttural taunt echoes in my thoughts as I take the hottest shower I can stand. Still wet, I creep into the bedroom and venture toward the dresser for a second time.

His clothing is exquisitely tailored, meaning only his shirts have any hope of fitting me. I settle on a white one and roll the sleeves up. The high collar disguises the worst of my neck, at least. My hair, however, is a hopeless cause that I tuck behind my ears, and my face can only be salvaged by wiping away the fresh blood and ignoring the bruising around my right eye.

It's only as I smooth the hem around my knees that I recognize the routine I've fallen into. Pretending. Perfecting.

Robert liked me properly dressed at all times outside of his room. He liked me to smile, and preen, and primp like the prettiest bird, happy in her cage. He'd hiss in disgust at the sight of me now: a bruised and broken plaything, bitten by another beast.

Here, there is no use pretending, and I let my hands fall with a sigh as I heed my captor's words.

I *explore*.

A part of me half expects to find the door to the room locked as I palm the handle. But, when I twist it slowly, it turns in my grip and I swallow hard. Beyond the door, I don't spy Mischa lurking in the hall.

In fact, it's empty, devoid of even his men. I don't cross a single soul as I creep toward the central corridor. Rather than savor my rare moment of freedom, I remember Mischa's command. *Have your run of the property.*

It's large, for one—overwhelmingly so. High, vaulted ceilings capture every sound made beneath them and throw them back ten times louder. I swear I can even hear my heartbeat mocking me in an unsteady echo. The air feels stale, untouched. As if no one has been here in ages, yet at the same time, everything has been meticulously maintained.

Does Mischa really live here?

I don't find any portraits on the walls to give me a clue. No photographs like the ones covering nearly every inch of the grand halls in Winthorp Manor, either. Robert Sr. took pains to ensure that anyone who entered his home knew just who had built it. Prestige and acknowledgment were everything. In the eyes of a Winthorp, being ignored was a fate worse than death, one saved for only the most worthless among them…

The feel of polished wood beneath my fingers draws my attention back to the present. Instinct must have guided me here without any input from my brain: I'm before a door. The one to Mischa's study.

Stick your nose where it doesn't belong.

With his taunt in my head, I hesitate for only a second before palming the handle and crossing the threshold. Everything looks untouched. Still, I circle the desk and wrench a drawer open for the hell of it. Do I expect to find anything of value? No.

But I can't ignore the thrill building in my stomach as I run my fingers through loose pens and scattered bits of blank paper. He's messy, forsaking the strict organization Robert prided himself on. My husband arranged his pens by nib color and size, preferring to have them lined up on the right-hand side of his desk, at the ready. He kept photos on the opposite end. Of me, of his father. He would look at either one depending on which mood he felt like embodying at that given moment: ruthless or vengeful? He could switch them out like hats.

Mischa keeps no such reminders, at least none I can discern. There are no trinkets, no keepsakes, no women—family or otherwise. Oh, but there have been. I picture the red room with renewed interest. Where would a heartless shell of a man keep reminders of his woman?

The answer is as intangible as it is obvious: *everywhere.* My perfume permeated Robert's suite. I may have been rarely seen and barely heard, but he was aware of my presence. *Always.* He relished in it: the captive bird whose chirping he could sense, no matter the room she was in.

Maybe the identity of Mischa's bird lurks in plain sight as well?

When I leave the study in search of another room, I find nothing in it. It's empty, decorated in muted grays, with no sign of life in sight. The room beside it reveals nothing, either. Neither do the rest in the entire wing. Retracing my steps back to Mischa's room feels like a halfhearted retreat to familiar ground—at least until I enter the room beside his.

My fingers tremble as I switch the light on and scan the interior for the second time. In the end, the perfume and the old clothes are my only finds. Mischa guards his secrets too well. He upholds his end of the bargain by letting me explore in peace, but I can sense him waiting deeper in the house for me to find.

I chase his essence down the grand staircase and then through an array of cavernous rooms. I suppose it's only fitting that I eventually spot his shadow in one of them, seated opposite an imposing man with dark hair. He's familiar, in fact, conjuring uneasy tension in my belly. *Sergei.*

"I came here alone, *Pakhan*," he says, conveying his chilling sense of calm. "I have no motive."

"With all due respect, I have to wonder why a man like you would want to waste good money on a Winthorp whore," Mischa replies.

Heart in my throat, I freeze, watching the exchange from the mouth of the hall.

"Waste? No." Sergei inclines his head dismissively. "Perhaps I want to *spare* the girl from whatever fate you have in store. After all, your hatred is toward the Winthorps themselves, is it not? I know the boy has contacted you about her—"

"Do you now?" Mischa counters, sounding unnerved in stark contrast to how I feel.

My blood runs cold. My heart stops. It takes me seconds to pick apart the cryptic riddle: the boy. *Robert?*

"I also know that you've refused him, despite what he offered. Why? Does revenge really mean so much to you? Or maybe there's some other reason you want to torment this woman—"

"Perhaps," Mischa admits. "Maybe I'm simply not finished with her yet."

"And when will you be? Finished?" Sergei counters. "Or have you lost yourself that much you can't even foresee an end to your brutality?"

"Careful, Sergei," Mischa says softly. "One might think you've forgotten the mission you yourself started. Have you forgotten Anna-Natalia already?"

"Never," the other man counters. "But I've lived long enough to learn that violence solves very little."

"And yet, you gave up your title as leader. Unless you've changed your mind?"

"No." Sergei leans forward, bracing his hands against the armrests of his chair. "Don't challenge me, Mischa. I meant no offense. But if you wish to keep the girl, it's your decision." He inclines his head respectfully before rising from the table. "You know how to reach me if you change your mind."

He turns for the door, spotting me there. His eyes scan my body slowly, honing in on my face with uncomfortable scrutiny.

"I can show myself out," he says to Mischa before advancing over the threshold.

I scurry back, pressing myself against the wall to clear enough space for him to pass. But he doesn't. He inclines his head instead, observing me more closely.

"What is your name?" He speaks softly enough that only I can hear.

I say nothing.

"Can you speak?" He frowns, gingerly swiping his thumb along my wounded cheek. "Your face... You look so much like—"

"Pardon me, Sergei," Mischa says, appearing in the doorway with his arms crossed. "I should keep better track of my toys."

"It is no trouble," Sergei replies, stepping back. "I was just curious if she had a name."

Mischa shrugs. "Not that I remember and not that it matters." He sounds casual enough, but his tone is harder than it should be. *Why?*

Perhaps for the same reason Sergei's eyes narrow ever so slightly, even as he maintains that calm smile. "Of course." He shifts his weight, appearing to turn. *Wham!* Something nudges my foot, throwing me off-balance, right into a wall of rigid muscle. Before I can attempt to regain my bearings, hot breath nudges my ear, carrying two grated syllables. "Elena?"

There's pain in that hollow tone.

And even more alarming...

There's recognition.

"Something wrong?" Mischa calls.

"My apologies," Sergei mutters as his hand settles over my shoulder.

"No. The apologies are *mine*." Another grip seizes my opposite forearm, decidedly harsher. "It appears she requires more training," Mischa says coldly, yanking me back before positioning himself in front of me. "I'll be sure to see to that."

Sergei says nothing. From my position, I can only hear his retreating footsteps, slow and hesitant. "Wait—" He speaks rapidly in a language I can't understand.

Whatever he says makes Mischa stiffen, his head tilted thoughtfully to the side. He's thinking, mulling something over. Then he shakes his head. "*Nyet.* She is not for sale."

Sergei laughs. "As you wish. My offer still stands if you change your mind."

He continues down the entire length of the hall. Before I can be sure that he's gone, I'm yanked off-balance and into a vacated room.

"What did he tell you?" Mischa demands.

My heart pounds out a frantic rhythm. Since my capture, I've never heard him sound like this. Guttural. Raw. On edge.

His eyes flash menacingly when I remain silent. "I won't ask you twice—"

"N-nothing," I insist.

"Oh?" His nostrils flare as if catching the stench of the lie in the air. "Then what did you say to *him*, Little Rose?"

I shake my head. "*Nothing.*"

"Then why did he just double his price for you?"

His price? Only now do I remember his earlier threat. *Someone offered to buy you...*

"Can you tell me why a man like Sergei Vasilev would offer two million for a Winthorp whore?"

My mind reels. Two million? Shocked, I have to force myself to reply, "I-I don't know—"

"If you fear me, then you should be terrified of Sergei. I've kept your soul intact." He tilts my chin, forcing me to meet his gaze, and nods. "It's still there. I've shown you far more mercy than you realize. But Sergei..."

There's a rare note of respect in his voice that triggers unease in my body. I picture the man from the night before, with his unrelenting calm and quiet power. Mischa not only respects him, he's *afraid* of him.

"Do you believe that men can change?" he wonders, pressing his thumb against my lower lip to demand an answer. "Do you?"

"N-no." If life with Robert taught me one thing, it was that men, of all creatures in this world, are the most set in their ways. The most stubborn. The most fearful of change. Poor Vanya seemed to be learning that the hard way, though I'm not stupid enough to mention that now. I simply nod against his palm. "They can't."

"Then you, my Little Rose, have a new monster to hide from. Sergei offered money for you, but that was just a formality. He can't demand you directly..." He stares beyond me, and I suspect he's speaking more to himself than anyone else. "But when he wants something, he gets it eventually—"

"Why would he want me?" An answer comes from the back of my mind before Misha can give me one. It's something Sergei himself said. *You look like her...*

"To fuck," Mischa suggests crudely. "To kill. Take your pick—"

"M-my mother." Pain constricts my chest. I can barely get my next words out. "Did…did he—"

"Rape her?" Mischa wonders. "Probably."

He makes the violent act sound so casual. And I look like her. Marnie. Sergei could have some sick fetish for reliving his abuse of her. Or…

"You're wondering if he could be your father?" Mischa asks, intruding upon my deepest thoughts without care or permission. "The timeline works, but from the rumors I've heard, your father could be any one of the men in the Vasilev employ."

Hot tears escape down my cheeks too quickly to attempt to hold back. Memories of my mother are like delicate shards of broken glass I've carefully preserved all these years. Beautiful to look at, painful to touch. I look like her, now more than ever, in a way Briar could only dream. Our scars are the same. Haunted, hollow, empty eyes.

"This hurts you," Mischa says.

I expect him to laugh, savoring my pain. Instead…his thumb catches a tear and smears it against the flesh of my cheek as if to ensure it was real.

"Knowing that your father could be one of them—"

"Stop."

"Didn't you ever question why she never told you?"

I did, only to conjure more pain whenever I felt heartless enough to mention it. "*Stop—*"

"If you had a child with me, and I let you run back to your precious husband. Would you ever tell her who I was?"

The question is as cruel as it is unbearable to contemplate. "No."

"Is that the same courtesy you extend to your child with Winthorp?"

Enough. I squeeze my eyes shut, slapping my hands over my ears. No. He can't pull this answer out of me. I won't let him—

"Look at me." His voice echoes inside my head, impossible to escape. "I won't tell you twice—"

"Just kill me." I utter the words while peeling my eyes open to gauge his expression. I find nothing. Not even hate. Just emptiness.

"This *is* killing you," he says. "Knowing that I can get inside your head. That I can take whatever the fuck I want—"

"Then take it!" I'm screaming though I don't know why. Or why more tears fall, coating my chin in wetness.

Robert is a parasite, feeding on whatever I have to give—but Mischa is a virus, invading every inch of me and turning my own body into a stranger's. Someone I hate.

"Or is torturing me how you ignore your own pain?" I wonder, knowing full well that it's already too late to turn back. "Number *seven?*"

I see black. Feel fire. Taste blood.

As I blink frantically, I realize I'm on the floor, staring up at the face of a monster. His fist is clenched, the knuckles dripping blood as my left cheek throbs in agony. His eyes are downcast, his mouth tight. In shock? Horror? His fingers flex, and for the first time, I see something I could describe as *human* in him.

Regret?

Regardless, I wait for my stomach to clench in fear and the cowering instincts I've lived by for so long to rear their head. Instead, my skin burns, set alight by shame and hate. *Hate.* I've never hated Robert. I loathe Mischa. The foreign emotion festers inside me, controlling my muscles and blotting out every intelligible thought.

With my head throbbing, I somehow make it onto my feet. Onto him, nails drawn, legs kicking, hands slapping, biting. Anything I can reach. I've played one game for so damn long that I have no patience for another.

If he wants to kill me, then he can kill me.

Now.

Another blow knocks me to the ground—his entire body. He pins me with his weight, using his hands to trap me beneath him. He's impervious to every blow I land. Kick after kick after kick. But he never retaliates.

He just shouts. Something my brain refuses to decipher. I don't want to hear him.

So I scream, aggravating my own eardrums. Like this, he can't reach me, not even when he wraps his hands around my throat and squeezes. Robbed of air, I choke. I wheeze.

And when he finally lets me go, I sob, shutting my eyes against his presence. He's still speaking. Still threatening. Still growling.

But I hear nothing. Just my own racing heartbeat and a jagged fragment of memory, repeating on a loop: *Elena. Elena. Happy birthday, Elena…*

Footsteps rattle the floor. Advancing? No, retreating.

He's gone—from the room at least. But, like any devastating illness, he lingers inside my head, and I'll go insane trying to keep him out.

CHAPTER 21

The memory is a cruel one, beginning the way the worst ones always do. With her.

Soft fingertips parted my hair in a gentle caress, coaxing me awake. "Happy birthday." The sweet voice sounded warmer than the purest ray of sunshine. So very beautiful. God, I'd give anything to hear it again... "My sweet girl," she murmured. "Already so big."

I peeled my eyes open, always in awe of her quiet beauty. Scars haunted her blue eyes, but I was young enough then to mistake them as a natural part of what made my mother so delicate. Her pain was a beacon, broadcasting to anyone and everyone the purity of her soul. It was the only thing of value she had left.

And for that reason, everyone wanted it.

"I can't stay long," she warned before pressing a kiss to my cheek. "I just wanted to wish you a wonderful day. Seven, already."

It sounded like such a prestigious age when she uttered it. Seven years. Seven long, painful years that had taken their toll on her youthful features. Only through memory can I track how she'd withered away right before my eyes. Her smile was fainter that day than any before it, shielding a million secrets I'd never learn.

"I have to go now." Noise in the hallway drew her attention and she hurried to her feet, smoothing the skirt of her dress.

Her visits had become less frequent by then. Sometimes days would pass without one. I'd only catch glimpses of her on my way through the halls as I assisted Martha, one of the servants. Always with Briar, her face turned away from me as though I didn't exist.

"Wait." A whine tugged at my voice, making her frown. "Please… can you sing it to me again? Just one more time?"

Her lips twitched, but with a wary glance over her shoulder, she returned to my side, placing her mouth near my ear. "Happy birthday to you. Happy birthday to you." Her fingers returned to stroking my hair, and I curled into her side, relishing the few extra moments of her attention. "Happy birthday, dear Elena. Happy birthday to you, my precious Rose…"

"Eat." His voice shatters the memory. The remnants of it cut into me—all of those questions I never asked. Like why she called me *Elena* only then, once a year, hidden away in a song.

Or why a monster would ever think to call me by it years after she's been gone.

"I said *eat.*"

Something clatters onto the floor by my side. A tray, I see once I peel my eyes open. It contains a sandwich and a bottle of water. I ignore them both by turning my face into the space between my raised knees.

As he has for what feels like an eternity, Mischa lingers for only a second before retreating from the room, slamming the door in his wake. I'm on a lower level. A basement, I think? Somewhere he dragged me after I attacked him. Newer memories meld with older ones, distorting the past few hours. Twenty…thirty?

Three days. I've been in this room for three days. It's starting to smell. *I'm* starting to smell. I'm starting to die.

My muscles ache, wasting away as my stomach protests days of hunger. My throat is so dry that each breath irritates my tender esophagus, but at least there's no moisture left in me to waste on tears. Without the fear of triggering any sobbing, I delve into those dark, deep memories I've left untouched for over sixteen years.

I chase my mother.

And she avoids me, even now, lurking in the depths of my psyche that hurt to reach.

I was her biggest secret, hidden away in a room at the very back of the servant's wing. I was her greatest treasure. Only now do I realize just what she left behind for me, as her legacy. The *real* reason why Robert Sr. reclaimed her, even after she'd been tainted by his enemy. Why Robert wanted me.

We look alike, after all. Our eyes were the same, well beyond any resemblance we shared with Briar. Our expressions were fragile, sporting tiny, hairline cracks. To monstrous men, those flaws glowed like tempting signs proclaiming, *I am weak. Break me. Destroy me.*

In the end, my mother destroyed herself in silence, with the aid of a razor blade and a running bath. By doing so, she passed her curse onto me. She revealed the only way out for someone like us: A doe can only survive at the mercy of a wolf for so long.

"Damn you, Eat!"

Another monstrous clang rouses me from my thoughts, but it's harder to leave my head for the real world. My eyes refuse to focus. It's bright. Someone turned a light on, illuminating my sparse surroundings and the concrete floor.

Four days. It's been four days since he brought me here when I refused to move from the pathetic puddle he'd left on the ground of the upstairs drawing room.

Four days since I stopped eating or drinking.

Four days since I first utilized the only gift my mother ever gave me: silence. She used it as a weapon, breaking it only on the rarest occasions, like my meager birthdays, honored once a year for just a few minutes at a time. Briar had parties. She had gifts beyond anything I could ever dream of receiving.

I had Marnie's love, the cruelest present of them all.

"Eat." Once again, Mischa's voice yanks me from the past. Or does he? Is he even here, or have I imagined him? My mother's face morphs into his, invading my one and only sanctuary. "Fuck —eat!"

Someone grabs my chin and pries my lips apart to shove a warm object between them. Something metal containing a liquid I let roll off my tongue, even as my stomach lurches in desperation. I taste nothing. Feel nothing.

Just...rage, so palpable that it stings like a physical blow.

"Damn you."

More wetness. Cold. When I don't swallow, a torrent of fluid drips down my nose and rolls down my chin.

Again, I'm left alone with Marnie. She doesn't acknowledge me, even now. She merely lurks around the edges of my consciousness, always out of reach. *Four days.*

The count remains the same when I'm disturbed by a soft hand brushing my cheek—not Mischa's. The fingers are too small. So is the face staring back at me as I force my eyes to focus.

No. Not her... Mischa is a cruel, unfeeling bastard. Hatred for him is the first tangible emotion I've felt in days. It burns through my sore, wasting limbs, too weak to direct itself toward anything in particular.

Nicolai's girl watches me with an unreadable expression. Her brown eyes stare blankly, even as she pats my chin and guides a utensil toward my lips with her free hand. A spoon.

The urge to refuse is nearly impossible to resist. I'm so close. Marnie feels nearer than ever. A few more days and I'd finally find her again. Touch her. Be near her with no one to come between us.

But guilt is a terrible, persistent thing. Marnie may have been immune to it at the end of her life, but I'm not. When the girl nudges my lips with the spoon, I part them and swallow the liquid gathered on it. My shriveled taste buds fail to discern a flavor. I just drink each mouthful woodenly, emptying the bowl. Upon setting it aside, the girl reaches for a bottle of water and silently urges me to finish it next.

Someone's cleaned her up and brushed her hair, having plaited it into two small braids. They dressed her as well, in a clean pink shirt and jeans. Vanya? Only he would be kind enough.

Has he sent her to me?

No. Most men aren't selfish enough to use a child to do his bidding—but a monster would be. Not even because he cared about my welfare.

He just wasn't finished with me yet.

When I gulp down the last drop of water, the girl gathers up the bowl and the bottle and exits the room, leaving the door open so that a sliver of light can penetrate my prison. It's a silent gesture that conveys an unmistakable request.

Four days of filth waft from my skin. What little waste I managed to expel is in a bucket in the corner of the room. Mischa never locked the door himself—my imprisonment had been self-imposed. Leaving now would be a harrowing defeat.

But if I don't, he'll send her again, forcing her to feed my emaciated frame.

Forcing her to watch me die.

With a groan, I unfurl my sore limbs. Weak with disuse, my legs refuse to fully support my weight. I have to cling to the wall with both hands just to rise to my feet, and leaving the room is a slow, painful ordeal.

Somehow, I make it up the stairs to the first floor. I pass no one, not even the girl. Not Mischa. I can't escape the feeling that he planned it, this silence that chases me through the halls and into the red room beside his.

I choose it solely for its familiarity. Nothing else.

After wrestling the door closed, I lock it. Then I stagger into the bathroom and lock that door as well. The sunken tub is a tempting escape. I draw the water scalding hot and collapse in the center of it, letting the warm wetness consume me.

How pathetic. I always thought I was above such an act: suicide. Marnie took her own life, but even after years of torment, I've never done the same. Not even when Robert showed me his worst. Not even when he made me wish for death.

I've never been desperate enough.

Or brave enough.

Am I now?

The answer eludes me as the water level rises. I lie here motionless, letting the moisture seep into my nostrils and lap at my parted lips. Just as my lungs start to burn, I tilt my head toward the ceiling and inhale the humid air.

Only now do I hear it. Thunder? No. *Pounding.*

In the end, I don't know how long it takes him to break the door down. He appears in the room amid a sound like thunder, his chest heaving, his eyes a flashing amber. He deflates when he sees me in the tub, still alive, his hands flexing in and out of fists.

Meeting his gaze, I force my dry, cracked lips to part and address him for the first time in days. "Mention my mother again and I'll kill myself." The falling water adds an ominous backdrop I couldn't have planned on my own to the threat. "You'll have to send my body back to Robert, still *his.* Always."

I'm dangling before him an object every monster covets: ownership. Does he want it?

His expression reveals nothing.

Robert would laugh at such an ultimatum. Then he'd drag me from the bath and show me just how many ways he fucking *owned* me.

Mischa? He meets my gaze and I shiver despite the steaming water basting my limbs. Four days have changed him almost as dramatically as they've affected me. Something cut his cheek, leaving three slender red lines slashed into the flesh. My fingers burn as if in guilt. Did I do that to him?

Darker stubble coats his jaw, contrasting with the sun-kissed gold of his hair. Dark shadows taint the skin beneath his eyes. From exhaustion? No... From brooding, smoldering rage. My punishment lurks behind those dangerous eyes. Soon, I'll feel it. Our dynamic of master and captive will be restored.

But for now?

He doesn't drag me from the tub. He doesn't say a damn word to me at all. He turns on his heel. He leaves, and he lets me have the one thing even my mother never gave me.

He lets me have one single round all to myself.

He lets me win.

CHAPTER 22

I lurk inside the red room, in self-imposed exile, while clues as to the goings-on of the rest of the manor's occupants seep through the door. Mischa's been busy, it seems. Shouts ring out from below as footsteps rattle the walls. Apart from a stern-faced man coming to replace the doors to the bedroom and bathroom, I'm left alone. The chaos rages around me like a storm, but I'm too tired to stick my head beyond the doorway and gauge its intensity. Instead, I sleep, savoring the precious hours of peace.

I bide my time.

Winning matters to men almost as much as their money does. Rarely do they lose their precious little games—and only when a greater prize is worth the forfeit.

So what is his end goal?

It terrifies me to admit the obvious: I don't know, and I can't even begin to guess.

Mischa's punishment lords on my horizon like a cloud, inescapable and building in strength with every passing second. How will he deliver it? With physical blows? With sex? By selling me?

The logical part of my brain does its best to muster up fear of any one of those scenarios. But it's no use. What little food I've ingested since leaving the basement doesn't return my itch for survival. I'm far too reckless when it comes to imagining what I can endure now.

A beating.

A rape.

Being whored out to other men.

None of those prospects inspire the terror they used to.

I'm too damn tired. I just want him to get it over with, whatever his plan may be.

But he's too damn patient.

When a knock rattles the door, he isn't the one behind it. Instead, I find Vanya, his expression wary. Balanced on his hands is another tray, this one containing a bowl of soup, a sandwich, and more water.

"Is...is something wrong?" I croak, alarmed by his serious expression.

"We will talk when you're feeling better," he says, his voice strained. "For now... Eat."

I take the tray from him without complaint, but he doesn't leave. Instead, he watches while I bring the food to the bed and force a few bites down. On behalf of Mischa or himself?

I can't tell.

Satisfied, he faces me directly, folding his hands over his lap. "I suggest you stay out of sight today. Mischa is planning—" He breaks off and seems to rethink his words. "Just stay out of his way."

"Why?" I can't stop myself from questioning him despite the part of me clenching in foreboding. Judging from the look in Vanya's eyes, whatever Mischa is up to, I don't want to know. "Is he planning to sell me?"

"Sell you?"

I'm caught off guard by how Vanya laughs.

"Things would be so much easier if he were, believe it or not."

I stiffen, but he doesn't sound malicious. Just...alarmed? "What is that supposed to mean?"

He meets my gaze. In the dim lighting, he looks so much older. Wizened and worn. "It means that you need to be more careful around him," he warns. "I won't pretend to know what you've been through before now. But Mischa... He can be a terrifying enemy. Or he can be a ruthless ally. If he sees you as a threat, he will eliminate you quickly." He frowns, eyeing me as if seeing me for the first time. His hand drifts toward my cheek only for him to lower it without touching me. "But if he sees you as a tool worth having, he will never let you go."

My brain mulls his words over, pairing them with the way Mischa cornered me in the bath, constantly weighing my worth to Robert.

I'm his enemy still. I'm sure of it.

So then why does Vanya's silence unnerve me as he leaves, closing the door behind him? Alone, I devour the rest of the food without dwelling on the tempting impulse to throw it away. When I finish, I leave the tray outside the door and climb onto the bed.

With Mischa's use for me in question, it's ironic that I've been forced to wear the strange woman's clothing once again. I chose a simple white dress that might have been a nightgown, yet I feel her in every inch of satin. She mocks me, this faceless predecessor. She taunts me.

You'll never know him.

Whoever she was, Mischa cared enough about her to save these delicate items of clothing. That act alone contrasts with everything there is to hate about him. It brought up an even more dangerous emotion: curiosity.

And, deep down, I know I've already learned far too much about my new monster.

I know what he feels like aroused.

I've tasted his rage.

As for his revenge…

It's dark when heavy footsteps approach the newly repaired door and give me an inkling of what lies in store for me. Unsteadiness. Each footfall scrapes the floor, slow and reluctant. The figure they belong to casts a wide enough shadow to blot out all light emanating from the hall. I'm bathed in darkness for so long that my eyes begin to adjust as the knob finally turns, revealing the creature lurking over the threshold.

Any hesitation he might have felt is left at the door. He strides boldly into the bedroom, slamming the door in his wake. The lock clicks and I watch him approach from the bed.

My stomach lurches as I spot something dangling from his right hand. Long. Thin…

Before I can name it, his knee extends, nudging me onto my side. My stomach. With me blinded, he mounts me from behind, ruthlessly using his weight to pin me in place. One of his hands cinches mine, wrapping something around my wrist. Rope? It bites into my flesh as he secures the limb beyond my head. To the bed frame? I tug it only to meet resistance.

With my thoughts still spinning, he does the same to the other.

And only now do I feel something: fear.

At his mercy, there is no escape.

I tense in anticipation as his hand grazes the back of my thigh and draws the hem of my dress up. Cold air kisses the flesh as if in warning: *Brace yourself.* He feels between my legs next, sliding what I suspect is the pad of a thumb along my entrance. Far too softly, so unlike his usual roughness. As if to spite me, he lingers there, testing me, and I can almost picture the thought circling his mind: hard or slow?

My punishment comes without delay. He chooses *both*. Every inch of his length slams inside me with no preamble. Stretching. Taking. Claiming.

Facedown against the sheets, I smother my moan into the silk.

Breathe, Ellen. After four choked gasps, I realize it's impossible. From this angle, he's deeper than he's ever been. Harder. Thicker. *Harsher.* The second thrust throws me forward, straining my binds and ramming the top of my skull against the headboard. My eyes shut as another gasp escapes my lips to sink into the sheets. Another. Another.

On the fifth brutal slam of his hips, real panic starts to gnaw away at the numbness. I can handle his hate. Or his lust. Not *this*.

Not silence.

He isn't frenzied, grunting with each thrust. He's slow. Careful. Precise. Each strike brutalizes a particular spot deep inside me that aches at the stimulation. It throbs. Heats. Ignites. The building pressure spreads through my belly, swiftly gathering in intensity until I'm moaning with every pass of his hips.

Robert fucked me only for his pleasure, taking what he wanted. Never *giving* this deliberate, callous…feeling.

I thrash, shaking my head, and buck against him desperate to arouse his rage.

Fuck me.

Hate me.

Knowing damn well how to attack, he *touches* me, sliding his fingers along the ridge of my entrance, above where we're joined. Too close. Too hard. Not hard enough.

Then he groans, smothering the sound against my ear. Words, I think. My brain struggles to interpret them.

"Bea..tiful. Fuck, you're beautiful—" Sharp teeth scrape the back of my throat and then bite down hard, grinding the flesh between them. *Take it.*

There is no reprieve. He rocks his hips, grinding the blunted tip of his cock against my abused walls. My eyelids flutter as my nails clutch at the air for stability.

I can taste his madness on my tongue. It grows more potent with every unsteady lurch of the bed and jolt through my core. Bit by bit, he loses that careful rhythm and just…punishes.

Slick flesh and sinful heat churn my thoughts into a senseless mass. Then, all at once, the harsh friction reaches a boiling point and every nerve short-circuits. Pleasure is a neutron bomb going off inside my skin. Muscles clench and tense, pulling him deep, deep, deep. Right when he begins to pulse inside me…

He wrenches himself out.

Fiery spurts of liquid splash against the backs of my thighs, and then he's gone. The mattress bounces as his weight withdraws. A metallic hiss betrays the sound of metal slicing through my binds, releasing me to lie here boneless and panting for breath.

He leaves me like that, huddled and used.

And, as the door slams, I begin to understand what other weapons he has in his arsenal besides physical violence.

He brings *pleasure.*

And, for the sake of my soul, I should fear every fucking drop.

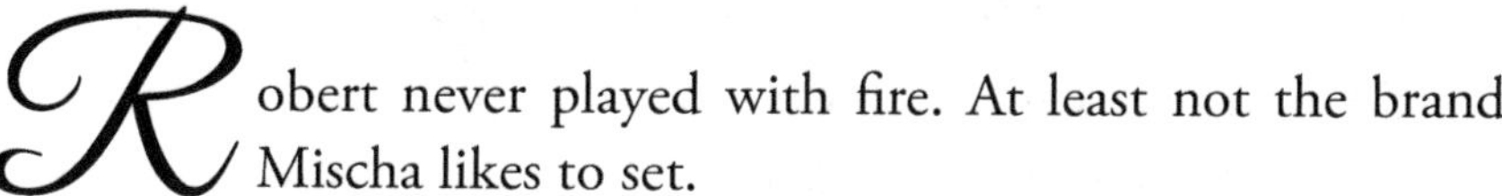

*R*obert never played with fire. At least not the brand Mischa likes to set.

Sex with my husband was an ordeal I knew how to cope with. I'd studied how to bear it.

I never dreaded it.

Five hours after he left, I know that my new tormentor will return. Soon. He'll do this to me again.

Will I let him? A shudder ripples through me; I've never contemplated such a thing before. Choice. I've never had to weigh the consequences of one action against the pain of another. In twenty-three years, I've *never* feared reaching my breaking point—not like this. I've never had to look in the mirror and wonder, *How much more can you take?*

The woman staring back at me doesn't seem to know. Her blue eyes sport visible cracks, splintering her stoic façade. Something terrifying lurks underneath those delicate features. I feel it running through my skin, causing my fingers to tremble against the countertop. In a desperate bid to suppress whatever it is, I draw another bath and scrub myself clean of every ounce of Mischa. When I return to the bedroom wrapped in a towel, I find another tray waiting for me on the bed.

I dress first, raiding the mysterious wardrobe for a modest black frock. Then I sip from a bowl of soup and obediently empty the accompanying water bottle.

After leaving the tray outside my door, I retreat within the room and wait. It should be a familiar game—the preferable option to any other. I used to wait for Robert without fail, anticipating his various moods to better withstand them.

I try to predict Mischa. I let the darkest depths of my imagination play with inventing the multiple scenarios he could have lying in wait, ready to spring. He could sell me to Sergei or return me to Robert alive. Any one of those outcomes would be better than the horrors my brain starts to conjure.

Him, returning to this room late at night with more rope.

Me, unable to stop him.

Not *wanting* to…

Suddenly restless, I rise from the bed and stagger to the doorway. My heart flutters at the thought of leaving my refuge. Regardless, I twist the knob and step out into the hall.

This part of the floor seems empty, but muted noise betrays a commotion lurking farther within the house. On bare feet, I find myself tiptoeing toward it. Why? I *know* what happens to those caught underfoot in the world of men. I also know just who most likely awaits at the heart of the tension resonating through the walls.

Like a moth to a flame, I can't escape the invisible shackle drawing me forward, anyway. Curiosity.

It feeds on the pathetic part of my soul that flares to life the moment I reach the stairs and spot the monster lurking at the base of them. His gaze finds me instantly, narrowing over my hiding spot in the shadows. God, his face looks even worse from this angle. The triplet slashes gleam in the glow of the overhanging chandelier, conjuring another memory from the depths of my psyche. Hellcat. *That's* what Robert's men called a "feisty" woman. *The bitch was a hellcat, fucking scratched me all up.*

They usually punished those women for their resistance. In my experience, hellcats wound up in the place of their namesake: hell.

Perhaps this is *my* tailored version of it? Trapped in his house, at his mercy, with no escape in sight. The flames are invisible, but the real burn comes from the deep-seated knowledge that I haven't tried to escape.

Not yet.

"Let's go." Turning from me, Mischa inclines his head, and only now do I notice the other men gathered around him. They crowd before the door and they leave in single file, their jaws clenched in stern determination, weapons in hand.

Something is wrong, and I recall a snippet of the conversation I overheard with Sergei. Robert? Could he be here? Now? My heart races at the thought. From *relief*. That's what I tell myself as I pick my way back to the red room and close the door.

I *want* my husband to find me. To save me? Something in my soul takes issue with that phrasing. I have to sink down, with my back pressed against the door, and find a new term to use. Find? Reclaim? Purify? Yes, I want my husband to *purify* me before Mischa's taint can take over.

As the daylight wanes, I let myself imagine how a reunion with Robert might unfold. He'd never storm into Mischa's compound on his own. No, a group of his men would do that. They'd be the ones to find me and drag me to the safety of Winthorp manor. He'd never consent to see me like this, so I'd have to be bathed first, have my wounds cleansed and all traces of another man erased. Only after Mischa's bruises have healed would he touch me again.

He would never knock.

But neither would Mischa.

The sound intrudes on the heavy silence, startling me to my feet. "Come in," I call out, expecting Vanya.

Hunched over and cautious, the older man enters my room—but a second is all it takes for me to register the features that don't belong to my kind benefactor. This man is taller. Older, even, with gray speckling more of his longer, darker hair.

And his eyes…

Unnervingly sharp, they hone in on me and narrow. "Don't scream."

I don't realize I've been on the verge of doing so until he advances, his hand outstretched, and the air dissipates from my lungs.

"Please," Sergei murmurs just loud enough to prevent being overheard by anyone in the hall. "I won't hurt you—"

"W-what do you want?" Instinct drives me back against the wall. My heart pounds as I struggle to take in as much of the intruder as I can. He's dressed in a dark suit, conveying a polished aura so different from the harsh one Mischa projects.

He sighs when I stiffen, shaking his head. "I want to talk," he says. "Alone."

"About what?"

You know what. I can't escape the suspicion that that's what he wants to say. His gaze is more piercing than Mischa or even Robert's. It penetrates my soul, slicing through my pathetic attempts to protect myself—but there's a softness to him my other tormentors lack. Even now, I can't deny that.

"Your mother was Marnie Winthorp," he says softly. "Wasn't she?"

My chest burns, and I can't stop myself from scanning the corners, hunting for Mischa. Is this another one of his games? He may be forbidden from using my mother against me, so perhaps he enlisted someone to do it for him?

But no. Only now do my ears register how he said that name. Reverently.

It's too terrifying a thought to consider. So I don't. "You should leave—"

"I won't upset you," Sergei says. "And I won't insult your intelligence by pretending that you don't know who I am. All I wanted was to give you this…"

He reaches into his pocket and a silver glint catches the light. Whatever he's holding is small, slender. A necklace?

"Here." He offers the object to me, clasped between his fingers. "Take this. And I don't know what Mischa's done to you or said —" He pauses as if waiting for me to explain, but when I say nothing, he sighs. "But know this: Whenever you need an ally, you come to me. No questions asked. No price to pay. You say my name and invoke my protection and no one will harm you. *Then* we will talk."

"W-why?"

A noise sounds from the hallway and Sergei cocks his head, frowning. "Remember that. Always. You have an ally in me."

He grabs my hand, shoving the hidden item against my palm. Then he turns to the door and is gone before I can choke a question out.

"Wait!"

Only silence greets me, and for whatever reason, I can't make myself move to follow him. The item was a necklace, I realize. It sparkles against my fingers, a delicate silver chain.

Dangling from the center is a small charm that somehow feels familiar, though I'm sure I've never seen it before: a small metal rose.

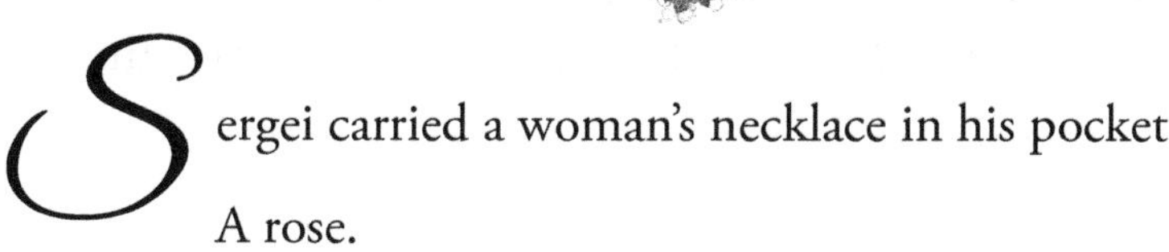

Sergei carried a woman's necklace in his pocket.

A rose.

My husband never plied me with jewelry. He dressed me in pretty silks and housed me in luxury—but, as Mischa pointed out, he never gave me a ring, or a broach, or a necklace. Is that a good thing? I have nothing here to remind me of him. Nothing but memories and this instinctive need to compare him to the man holding my figurative chains now.

Robert would never leave me unguarded like this.

He would never scar me publicly so that the world knew his claim.

But for what reason?

Paranoia keeps me awake. I twist Sergei's necklace around my fingers until something makes me creep toward the vanity and place the chain against my throat. It settles there uncomfortably, like a missing piece I'd never realized was gone. My hands shake as I fasten the clasp and let the rose charm hang against my collar.

It's as if the charm is magic. My resemblance to Briar is all but gone. I look more like another person now than ever. Minus my scars, we could be the same haunted woman.

Marnie.

Trapped in Sergei's grasp, did she huddle in her prison and wait for the end of her nightmare? Of course she did.

But I can't. I won't.

For once, my mantra feels meaningless. *Breathe, Ellen.* But for what? To stay alive at Mischa's demand? To follow even further in Marnie's footsteps?

To die alone.

To live in a cage.

To remain a selfish, captive bird.

I can't.

So I *stop* breathing and hold my breath as I creep to the door and press my ear to the wood. It's silent, but something won't let me grasp the handle. Mischa isn't foolish. I'm sure he has his men watching the doors, just in case.

So I turn to the windows and shrug aside the heavy drapes shrouding them. I didn't notice before exactly where this room is positioned. Below stretches a wide field, and ivy creeps up a stone façade. The rusted latch squeals as I test one of the panes, but they open smoothly only to present a stark reality. Over a full story off the ground, I either have to jump or climb.

Shadows shroud the type of surface waiting down below. Stone? Earth? The more I contemplate my options, the more escape feels like a cruel whim than an attainable reality. Tears prickle behind my eyes. It's no use.

Or is it?

I find myself observing the ivy again and brush the tip of a plant with my fingers. It's rooted firmly to something I didn't notice before: an iron lattice strong enough to support my weight. Or at least I hope as much as I climb onto the sill and brace one of my feet in the gaps. Tentatively, I sink down and nearly sigh in relief as the support holds.

Without stopping to acknowledge the consequences, I guide myself lower, clinging to whatever part of the lattice I can reach. I'm slow. Too slow. Noises of the night echo, but it's impossible to decipher if they belong to woodland creatures or Mischa's men.

But there's no turning back now.

I keep going, forcing myself to climb until my bare foot brushes what feels like packed earth. Up above my window glows, a beacon in the darkness. How long until Mischa comes for me? Minutes? Seconds?

There isn't time to plan. I set my sights on a copse of trees in the distance and run. An icy wind nips at my skin and tears at my hair. It's like the earth itself is cackling at my futile attempts. *He'll find you, Ellen. He'll find you.*

Deep down, I think a part of me knows that. I keep running anyway, letting my surging pulse spur me on. Branches and dried leaves crunch underfoot. It's bitterly cold, and my breaths paint the air in tufts of white.

But I keep running.

Defying.

Breaking…

Sergei's necklace hammers my chest with every sprint, and I can't get his face out of my head. Hers. Did she resist him? Fight him? Hate him?

Was he the reason she was burdened with me?

Suddenly, the ground changes beneath my feet. My heel slips over a slick patch of mud and I trip, landing on my knees, tasting dirt. It's so silent here. Too silent. All I hear are my own frantic breaths and… Noise?

Faint. Rapid. *Footsteps*, heading right for me.

Gasping, I scramble to my feet, knowing in my soul that it's no use. He's too fast, crashing through the trees near my right. I can't get my bearings. The air changes. Shadows shift underfoot.

Wham!

I'm struck so hard that I go sprawling and there's nothing I can do but brace. Groaning, I rise to my knees, making a note of my surroundings. Faint moonlight illuminates a stark landscape of winding hills and looming trees.

Then nothing. Whether by the grace of God or accident, I tripped mere paces from a sharp drop. The earth gives way to a cliff that overlooks looming darkness.

And makes for the perfect trap.

Leaves rustle nearby, and I lurch to my feet, squaring my stance. To fight? God, I don't know. Maybe I will. At least this time I won't let him corner me like an animal. When footsteps near my position, I turn to face him, hunting his form in the darkness. Sure enough, I spot a breathless figure crouched nearby.

But their shape is wrong. Too small. Too slender. And their face…

Graced by a beam of moonlight, pale skin glows, delicate and pure. Wide, blue eyes gleam in a face so familiar that it's like looking into a mirror—an enchanted one that shows my reflection as it once was, free of scars and bruises. The shocked expression even matches mine, I'm sure.

But then my doppelganger's eyes narrow in recognition, and pink lips form a voice much more charming than mine. "Ellen?"

Numb with shock, all I can croak is, "Briar?"

She's still so beautiful. Is that what shocks me the most? Huddling under the threat of Mischa, it was easier to ignore the damage done to me then. Not now, with a perfect version of my features forming a stark contrast.

She's still wearing silk, her hair slicked back into a neat bun. So polished, in fact, that she could have come from a ball or gala.

Not a madman's backyard.

I've gone insane. That explains it. Still, I find myself talking to what must be a figment of my imagination. "What are you doing here?"

The mirage of Briar blinks, startled. Then…she throws her head back to display her pale throat and laughs. She's loud, no doubt catching notice for miles—but that's not what makes my stomach sink. It's the coldness reflected in her gaze as she meets mine directly.

"I fucking knew it," she hisses, her hands clenching into fists. "That bastard. I fucking knew it!"

"Knew what? How did you get here?" A sudden thought takes my breath away. "Did Mischa—"

"I should have known he'd do anything to have you back." She takes a step back, still laughing. Lost in amusement, she doesn't seem to realize just how close she is to the ledge. Her heeled feet kick up loose rocks that clatter into the abyss. "I was hoping you would just stay gone. Why couldn't you?"

Once again, I'm not sure if she's really here or a hallucination. A nightmare. In twenty-three years, I've never heard her sound so lost. Or so damn cold.

"What are you talking about?"

"Seriously?" She cocks her head. "You're *still* so fucking stupid." One of her hands drifts to her cheek, brushing the unblemished skin. "They really thought you were me…"

I copy her, flinching as my palm grazes my injured cheek.

"Why couldn't you just keep your mouth shut?" Briar wonders so softly that I barely hear her. "Did you really think he'd save you? No!" Her voice rises in pitch, alarmingly loud. "I won't let him use me as his fucking pawn—"

Above her shouting, I almost miss it: the earth crunching—warning of the approach of a larger creature. I smell him before I even see him, so potent that it chokes me. Raw strength. Unbridled rage.

Mischa.

Briar doesn't notice him until he's already stepped from the cover of a nearby tree. Her skin goes even paler, her legs trembling.

But she isn't the figure caught by the full force of his gaze. He doesn't say a word, but his posture reminds me every bit of a hunter's. Waiting for me to move. To run.

"Stay away from me!" Briar staggers wildly, her arms outstretched. Her foot catches a stray branch, sending her stumbling.

I race for her without realizing, grabbing her arm. "Stop—"

"Let go!" She flails and her hand connects with my chest, knocking me back.

I careen against a firm surface. *Mischa.* He grabs my waist to steady me but shoves me aside. I can only stare as he moves with predatory grace, lunging for Briar.

"No!" I strain for them, but the terrain is too uneven. I can't regain my balance and my fingers grasp at muddied earth. Then air.

What must take seconds feels like an eternity of falling... Eyes shut, I brace for the end that I'm sure is coming. *Wham!* I feel it: sharp, unrelenting pain searing through my shoulder. From above?

"Fuck! Give me your other hand."

Dazed, I look up. Thick fingers encircle my wrist, belonging to a figure hunched over the cliff, his eyes like fire.

Mischa.

"Give me your other fucking hand!"

I try, straining my fingers through the air. But his are too far away. My legs kick at nothing. His grip is slipping...

"Don't let me go." I don't even know why I beg. Because he will go after Briar. I can sense the hesitation in how his eyes cut to his right. He shifts his posture, adjusting his grip and my heart sinks. "Don't!"

Agony rips through my shoulder as I'm suddenly yanked higher. Wet earth scrapes along my flesh. Solid ground. Looking up, I see Mischa hunched over and panting. I barely register the look in his eyes. Relief?

It's only there for a second before his hand curls into a fist. I hear the sickening blow as white dots explode across my vision.

Then darkness.

Pain.

And silence.

'm home. Either that or dead. Only in heaven or hell could the air be so still and the world so quiet. Silk sheets chafe against my skin, and it's painfully easy to picture what will await my eyes when I dare open them.

White walls.

A canopy.

My old cage.

Already, my capture lurks nearby, tainting my reality with his scent. Male. Unbearable. My lips flutter to put a name to him. "R-Robert?"

But Robert never smelled like blood.

"No," my captor replies. The voice. The accent. They tether me in place more securely than physical binds ever could. "Guess again, Little Rose."

My eyes open, but the reality facing me isn't the one I pictured. These walls are red. Heavy drapes shield the windows, and a lone figure lurks in the corner. His hair is unbound, partially shrouding his face. The only hints of his expression I can make out are a stern, clenched jaw and hollow eyes.

"W-what happened?" I croak, though the question is merely a formality. It's like we're following a script, he and I. I feign ignorance while he smothers with rage, ready and willing to exert his authority.

"You tried to run away, Little Rose," he says, crossing his arms over his chest. Mud and leaves cling to his fatigues and I remember.

Running. Falling. Briar…

My heart is throbbing. I cradle it in both hands, desperate to make sense of my thoughts. Sergei came to visit me. Like a fool, I escaped. I ran. But, of all people, I ran into my sister?

"You hit your head pretty hard," Mischa warns. "Hopefully there is no permanent damage—"

"You went after me," I whisper, ignoring every instinct in my body warning me to stay silent. "Not Briar. Why?"

"Hmm?" He cocks his head. "I don't know what you're talking about, Rose. There was no one else. Just you. This property stretches for miles. Tell me, what would Briar Winthorp be doing so close?"

My heart beats frantically in my chest, picking up on the suspicion lacing his tone. Is he being serious? Or merely trying to confuse me?

Groaning, I dig my thumbs at my temples. "My head hurts—"

"Drink." He nods his chin toward the nightstand.

I spot a tray waiting there, complete with a glass of water. Sitting upright, I grab the drink and drain it, never taking my eyes off him for a second.

Laughing, he basks in the attention. I jump when he starts to advance. Only now do I notice the vibrant, red substance painting the flesh from his nose down to his jaw.

"You're bleeding."

He frowns at the sound of my voice, weak and hoarse. Almost like I really give a damn.

But I don't.

More memories return in painful snippets, demanding my attention. "Briar. Where is she—"

"Tell me. What did we decide on, Little Rose?" Mischa wonders as one of his hands feels along his thigh. With predatory grace, he slides his fingers into the pocket of his fatigues and withdraws something long. Gleaming. "That's right. You want to be sliced into pieces." He feigns ignorance as he hefts the blade for inspection. "Think. If I were to give you the choice right now between a permanent divorce or severing that pretty head from your body, which would you choose?"

He seems to think it's a serious question, one that requires ample thought and consideration. But it doesn't.

"I'd want you to kill me."

"Oh?" He laughs, spitting more blood down the front of his shirt. "Are you sure about that, Little Rose? No. I think you want to live. Badly enough you'd *beg* for it."

My eyes go to the knife. His fingers twitch over the handle, tightening, relaxing…tightening, relaxing. Clenching. For a second, I'm back in the woods, dangling by a thread. *Don't let me go!*

"Are you just going to watch, Little One?" he asks, drawing my attention back to his face. He watches me coldly and jerks his chin toward the door to the bathroom.

I recognize the silent command. Not from Robert this time. Briar used to issue the same order whenever I found her hidden away in a room with a knife to her wrist. She never cut deeper than the surface layer of skin. Just enough to bleed. Her blue eyes would meet mine without a shred of concern and she'd always nod, merely once, when found. *Clean me up.*

Silently, I climb from the bed and smooth out the skirt of my borrowed dress. As my bare feet brush the tiled marble of the bathroom floor, I realize I'm limping.

"Your legs aren't broken," Mischa remarks as if in afterthought, but I catch him watching me, hunting my every step. "But you'll bruise."

Bruises deep enough to ache with every step I take. Even so, I make it into the bathroom alone. After spotting a shelf of linen, I grab a washcloth and wet it beneath warm water from the sink.

When I return to Mischa, he cocks his head back, directing with his gaze where I should clean first. His *chest*, not his face. Someone hit him there, drawing a stream of blood from his nose and splitting the upper lip. He'll heal with a bruise, but nothing more.

Below his collar, however, someone struck him with a knife. From a layer of rent cotton, I can tell that it's deep. He'll have another scar to add to his collection.

"What happened—"

"Your husband," he says, gritting his teeth against the pain. "Did you ever see him wear a ring? You don't."

I glance down at my naked fingers and swallow my instinctive answer back. My husband didn't need a ring to own me. "Yes," I say instead, picturing the silver ornament my husband was rarely without. "He wears the Winthorp insignia on his right hand." It was an ironic signature for such an infamous family. Beautiful, even: a dove carrying a delicate blade between its talons.

"So you'd recognize it," Mischa says, almost to himself. The movement must irritate his wound, because he sucks in a breath and snaps his fingers.

Obediently, my free hand drifts to the hem of his shirt, aiming to help him remove it, but he shakes his head, clenching his jaw. So I press the cloth against the wound over the fabric and hold it there. He hisses but then grinds his teeth to suppress even that much sound. After a few seconds, he bats my hand away and grabs the cloth himself.

"I don't dole out second chances, Little One," he says, ignoring how fresh blood begins to taint the white fabric between his fingers. "But ignorance is bliss. So, this time, I'll let you make an educated decision."

I flinch as he lifts the knife only to return it to his pocket. Before I can deflate in relief, he takes something else from his pocket. Something small. Bloody. It leaves a smeared trail of burgundy as it lands on the sheets before me.

"Do you want to die as Ellen Winthorp or become someone new? Either way…" He stands and approaches the door while I observe the small object he left behind, attempting to identify it. It's round. Shiny. Metal?

"Your husband is dead," Mischa tells me at the exact moment I recognize the item as a ring. One I only ever saw on one man's finger. "I suggest you plan your future as a widow carefully."

A thud echoes as the door slams in his wake.

Or does it?

Perhaps the thunderous sound is just my heart stopping? I'm on my knees, clutching fistfuls of the sheets in search of stability I'll never find.

There is no mistaking that ring.

There is no ignoring the blood.

There's no escaping Mischa.

Your husband is dead.

And so am I.

CHAPTER 23

obert Winthorp is my identity, and he never needed a shiny diamond trinket to prove it. He adorned me with blood instead. With wounds, and scars, and terrifying marks on my psyche that could never be symbolized by something as frivolous as a ring. So how ironic is it now that one of his is all I have left of *him*?

I can't touch it. I can't take my eyes off it, either. It speaks to me. I hear it hissing a vow to my very soul: *I fucking own you, Elle.*

A shadow falls over me, darkening the scarlet sheets clenched beneath my fingers.

"H-how?" I don't even have to turn to know just who I'm speaking to. Mischa couldn't leave me alone for long.

No, he couldn't resist. He had to watch. Whether he saw Robert's demise with his own eyes or not, it wasn't enough. After all, he warned me himself: This…this is how he wants to see my husband die.

In my eyes.

"How did you kill him?" I rasp, repeating the question when he hasn't given me an answer. I can't look at his face. The ring has my sole attention. Even now, Robert commands obedience. "Tell me how—"

"Do you really want to know the answer?"

I flinch at something I find in his tone—mainly what I don't: there's no mocking in it. He's tired. He's on edge. *He's not lying.*

"All you need to know is that the fucker's dead, and you're running out of time to decide whether or not you want to join him."

My heart falters, but not out of fear. Burning tears well from my eyes, spilling down my cheeks as hot as blood. Are they for Robert? Maybe. Maybe not. Perhaps they're more selfish than anything else. Ellen Winthorp dies in an instant and it hurts. There's no one there to mourn her. Just a monster who watches her agonizing end without a shred of mercy to spare.

"Why?"

For once, I've given him a question he doesn't know how to answer. "You know why—"

"No." I shake my head, still transfixed by the tiny sliver of metal resting on the bed. "Not that. I want to know *why*. Why you hate the Winthorps. Why you—"

"You have a lot of demands for a dead woman." There's nothing to temper the threat in his voice. His tone falls flat as the usual fire is extinguished from that piercing gaze. Left behind is a hollow mask, and for the first time, I'm faced with the *real* Mischa: a creature without a shred of humanity to hide behind.

His accent takes over. Was he even speaking English in the first place, or had I conjured up some semblance of intelligible words in the grated series of growled syllables? "I guess you've made your fucking choice."

He advances a dangerous step, but I don't cringe back. Not even when I focus my blurred vision in his direction and meet his gaze fully.

"Tell! Me! Why!" I hardly recognize the shouting woman who utilizes my body to speak. I've only heard her once before, the same night he went too far and slandered my mother's name. "What did they do to you?"

"You want to know?" He snatches the bloodied cloth from his chest and throws it at me. Rage disrupts its aim and it smacks off the wall, inches from my head. Gritting his teeth against any pain, he wrenches his shirt over his head and turns, revealing the mangled flesh of his back. "You really want to know? Twenty-four years ago, your precious Robert and his fucking father had a plan to end the feud, you see. They meant to take my father but changed their target at the last minute. They took me and my mother instead. They locked us in a cage and placed bets on which death would matter more."

His vile words paint the scene for me. I see it. I see him. He had to be young. Twenty-four years.

"Robert would have been a child—"

"A child?" He sneers at the word, meeting my gaze from over his shoulder. "I don't think you've ever met a fucking child, Ellen Winthorp. They lined my mother and me against the wall of their fucking dungeon and told me to choose. Your child of a husband gave me my options, barely as old as I was."

Eight, to be exact. Robert would have been eight. The Winthorps rarely displayed pictures of themselves as children, but I have no trouble imagining him: a beautiful boy with golden curls and soulless, brown eyes.

"He told me to choose who would die. Me or my mother?" Mischa's voice deepens, straddling the rasping edge of a growl. "They wanted me to pick but she…she made the choice for them. She begged for my life. So—" He breaks off, staring through the walls of the manor and into the past. "They made her watch them carve their mark into my back." He extends his arm behind him, tracing the rough tip of the scar along his spine. "They made her watch them beat me within an inch of my life. And then they gave her a gun and told her I would only live if she made *me* pull the trigger—"

I can't hear this. My hands claw at my ears, but he's there to wrench them away, ensuring I hear every word he has to say.

"Her fingers shook, but I was too weak to pull away. She died with her brains in my lap, you little cunt. And then I had to watch the rest of my fucking family, picked off one by one. You ask why I hated your husband?" He shoves me back so hard that I fall to my knees. "That is why. But *you* disgust me more than that piece of shit. He knew what he was. You're just a pathetic bitch, clinging to his shadow. So I'll ask you now. Who do you want to be?" He drops something down in front of me. The knife, its edge mocking and bright. "Ellen Winthorp? Or the bitch *he* never let you become?"

He kicks the blade closer to me when I don't reach for it. Then he sinks down, caging my body against the floor with his own. Thick, wet fingers fist through my hair, using it as a tether to force me to face him.

I'm sobbing, gasping and moaning through waves of tears. For Robert? For me? There's no end to the grief, yet it has no true purpose. It just consumes, like fire.

"Decide," he snarls.

What?

Terror rips through me as he captures my hand against his palm, forcing my grasping fingers to scrape the carpet, grabbing something solid. It's hard, conforming to my grip. I identify what it is without even having to look down: the knife. It's almost too big for me to handle with one hand. Too heavy. It takes two tries before I can lift it and eye the beautiful, lethal edge.

"You think you can kill me, Little One?"

I've pointed the blade at him without realizing.

Laughing, he tightens his grip and lowers the tip toward another target. "I'll give you the same choice your husband gave my mother," he explains. "Decide who you want to kill. The part of you that belongs to him?" He applies enough leverage to force the sharpened tip to kiss the flesh of my forearm. "Or the small, pathetic piece of you he never managed to touch?"

Oh. My free hand trembles against the floor. Reaching around me, he seizes my wrist and tilts it, exposing where the veins lie. Instinctively, my naked ring finger flexes, sensing the imminent danger.

"Do it," Mischa commands. "Make your choice. Or are you so fucking weak you'll die completely for him?"

He lets me go, leaving my trembling hand to hold the knife alone. It twitches in the air, wavering toward various directions.

Him. Me. The floor.

Back again.

"Do it," Mischa goads, his mouth near the nape of my neck. There's no fear that I might turn on him again. The enemy he's presented is far more formidable than he will ever be: myself. "Do it!"

The blade falls, cutting side down, and pain explodes through my entire being. White. Endless…

Through a haze of tears, I see red. Red floors. Red walls. Red, painted skin.

My heartbeat surges, forcing hammering blood through my veins. With the scent of salt tainting the air, Mischa's grating voice is my only anchor to sanity.

"Keep going," he says thickly. "Do it. Do it!"

But I don't even know where exactly the knife continues to strike.

Or, in the end, which part of me is cut away.

Rose? Ellen?

Regardless, one woman dies in the fiery torrent of blood and agony.

And she doesn't even scream.

SAMPLE OF VII...

Dying to know what happens to Ellen and Mischa?

Would you like a sample of VII?

Grab your sample now!

WAR OF ROSES SERIES
EXTENDED EPILOGUE

Do you want more of Mischa and Ellen? Join my newsletter to enjoy the War of Roses Extended Epilogue Series!

https://www.lanaskybooks.com/newsletter

A WORD FROM THE AUTHOR

Hey there!

Thank you so much for reading! If you enjoyed the story, please leave a review and recommend the book to any friend you think would love this twisted world. You'd have my eternal gratitude. Even a short sentence goes a long way!

Then, come join the rest of us dark romance lovers in my Facebook Group where you can get snippets, sneak peeks of upcoming books and even help vote on aspects of future novels.

Come to the dark side:
https://www.facebook.com/groups/lanasbeautifulmonsters/

WANT MORE STUFF TO READ?
Join my newsletter and get a **free book**! Plus, you get to stay updated with any new releases, random giveaways and exclusive sneak peeks!
https://www.lanaskybooks.com/newsletter

Other Novels: https://lanaskybooks.com/

FREE BOOK - JOIN MY NEWSLETTER

Dark, Twisted Romance

Join my newsletter and get a **free book**! Plus, you get to stay updated with any new releases, random giveaways and exclusive sneak peeks!

https://www.lanaskybooks.com/newsletter

ABOUT THE AUTHOR

Lana Sky is a reclusive writer in the United States who spends most of her time daydreaming about complex male characters and parenting her Cockapoo Joey. She writes dark, twisted romance across several genres. Her titles include everything from mafia romance to vampires.

facebook.com/AuthorLanaSky

twitter.com/lanasky101

amazon.com/author/lanasky

pinterest.com/lanasky101

goodreads.com/lanasky

instagram.com/lanasky101

bookbub.com/authors/lana-sky